NENE CAPRI

PRESENTS

THE MAGIC WAND

A NOVEL BY:

N. TROUBLE

Copyright © 2018 Nene Capri Presents

The Magic Wand by N. TROUBLE

Nene Capri Presents Publishing, LLC
PO Box 743432
Riverdale, GA 30274
770-515-9164
nenecapripresents@gmail.com

Late Night Lick: The Magic Wand is a work of fiction. Names, characters, places, and incidents either are products of the author's imagination or are used fictitiously, and any resemblance to actual persons, living or dead, business establishments, events, or locales are entirely coincidental.

Cover Design: by Lashonda Johnson & Nene Capri NeneCapri@gmail.com & Ghostwriterinc2016@gmail.com

Book Interior Design by Lashonda Johnson Ghostwriterinc2016@gmail.com

Chapter One

Wet and Wild

The sounds of tiny specks of rain, could be heard tap dancing off the windshield, in between *Migos* verbal assault on *'Too Hotty'*, and the slurping of Maxine's mouth engaging in oral love making. Her sweet mouth expanded simultaneously as his dick swelled. Drool spilled from the side of her mouth, dripping down his brown shaft, settling between his sack and his thighs. She quickly popped his steal from her mouth making a loud, *'THUCK!'* noise.

Maxine, hungrily used her warm tongue and sweet lips to vacuum the spit from its landing pad. Making small circles on his inner thigh, then sucking his right testicle. She used her tongue to twirl it around in her mouth.

Kareem, opened his eyes wanting to witness the job. To his surprise her green intoxicating stare glared back at him, causing his dick to get harder. She rubbed his dick against her gorgeous face and cuddled it as if it was a cashmere pillow, instead of his ten and half inch dick.

She closed her and whispered, "I love this dick."

Kareem, ignored the rubbish coming out of her mouth and grabbed a handful of honey blonde hair, forcing his dick back into her young sweet mouth. Maxine's pussy continued to thump. A devilish grin plastered across her face. As she removed his hand and rapidly bounced her head up and down, devouring as much dick as her sweet mouth allowed. Before he could cum, she snatched his dick out of her mouth, opened the car door, and jumped out.

"What the fuck?" cursed Kareem.

"Come on, come get this pussy." Maxine ordered, walking to the hood of the 8 series BMW.

The rain picked up, instantly drenching her one-piece Tom Ford mini skirt. Kareem, shook his head as he watched her cat crawl up the hood. She spun around and spread her legs open on the windshield, giving him a view of her neatly shaved pussy. A small patch of honey blonde hair, revealed her true hair color. Her small fingers slid up and down her pussy, as she rotated her hips in an effort to cum faster. Kareem stroked himself while giving her eye contact.

"You cheating, you don't want this pussy?" Maxine taunted.

A car slowly drove by giving her the audience she yearned. The already tight one-piece hugged every curve of her body. Her nipples darted out from her naturally perky breasts. Maxine, loving the taste of her own juices, licked her fingers until the creamy fluids disappeared.

Kareem suddenly feeling challenged, exited the car. Kareem was handsome, with light brown-skin, standing five-feet, ten-inches tall, weighing approximately one hundred, ninety pounds of solid muscle, and built like an NFL strong safety.

"You want me to come get that pussy, huh?" He grabbed her wrists, spinning her around.

Maxine slid to the front of the hood, reaching for the love of her life.

"Nah, don't touch me." Kareem warned, smacking her hand away, causing her to pout. Her lips poked out inviting his kiss.

Kareem, rubbed his dick against her dripping pussy, as their tongues wrestled. Then grabbed her thick legs and wrapped them around his waist. At the feel of his entrance, Maxine nearly lost her breath. No matter how many times they'd had sex, her small tight tunnel, could never get used to his size.

Kareem, pushed her down on the hood, using her tiny waist to navigate their movement. No longer in pain, Maxine, pinched his nipples through his dress shirt. Kareem deepened his thrusts, pushing his entire dick inside her sweet pussy.

"Oh shit, yes, damn babe fuck this pussy." Maxine cried out.

Kareem, held his stroke deep and hard before making his dick bounce inside her.

"Owww! Yes, oww…hmmm." Maxine squeezed him tight feeling the muscles in his back bust out of his shirt.

Kareem locked in, closed his eyes, and stroked her dripping wet pussy long and hard. He pulled most of his love muscle out, leaving just the head in, rotating his hips in a circular motion, then driving his large dick back into her pussy slow and hard.

"Hmm oh, yes…fuck me…this is my dick. Give me all my…oh my…give me all my dickkk... Damn, I love it when you do the round-n-round." Maxine, praised

The lights of an approaching car, signaled Kareem to speed up.

"Don't rush baby, let them watch!" Maxine ordered.

Kareem begged to differ, not only had he been ready to cum, but he had somewhere to be. As he speeded his thrusts, she leaned forward clasping her arms around his neck, bucking up and down his long thick dick like a mad woman.

"Yes. Yes. Ow…yes! Make me cum babe."

The car beeped its horn, slowed down, and rolled down the window. "Get a room, I'm calling the police!" yelled an older white lady.

"Darling leave them alone." her husband fussed, then he leaned over his wife, and yelled, "You only live once, put it down for a retired stud." Then rolled up his window and continued watching the show.

"Watch out for that parked car idiot!" yelled his wife.

Maxine came all over Kareem's dick, then tightened her muscles, making him instantly return the favor. His knees buckled causing him to lean forward, she squeezed him even tighter.

"You know your young ass crazy, right?" Kareem asked, removing hair from her eye.

"Nah, you make me crazy. Plus, I know I'm not the only one, so I have to be the best."

"You sure know how to fuck the mood up don't you?" Kareem started fixing his clothes as the rain stopped.

"What? I'm just speaking the truth. You been home what eight months? How much longer are we going to sneak around?"

"*Sneak around?* We down the street from your condo, having sex outside, in the rain, on top of my beamer. This what you call sneaking around?"

"You know what I mean. That lady keeps asking questions. I want to tell her."

"No, what I tell you?" Kareem, grabbed her by the bottom of her chin and squeezed her face.

"Stop, you're hurting me." Maxine, whined as tears appeared.

Kareem quickly moved his hand, his lips caught each tear, as they rolled down her pretty face. "I'm Sorry."

"It's not supposed to be like this. I did everything for you, visits, money, pictures. I even sacrificed my freedom, and career by bringing you drugs to sell. She left you, but I have to hide our relationship? You can't blame it on my age, I'm a twenty-five years old grown ass woman."

"Look, give me some time, I got you. This don't have shit to do with her. Fuck her, she left, you rode out. Get in the car, we can talk about this another time." He grabbed her hand and walk her to the passenger side.

Opening the door for her, he couldn't help but notice how she'd became an overnight social media sensation. At five-feet-two, she was thick, with a tiny waist, a natural fat ass, and big, perky breasts.

Once she got comfortable sinking in the heated leather seats. Kareem, stepped around the back of the car. He popped the trunk, retrieved a shopping bag, then entered the driver's side, and dropped the huge bag on her lap.

"I brought you something."

"For me?" She anxiously tore into the bag, finding A Swankier Duffle bag by *Louis Vuitton*.

"You can use it for your work clothes and stuff. I know you be struggling with three bags."

"Thanks baby, I really needed this." She leaned over and gave him a big kiss on the cheek. "I'm still mad though."

"I know." The trunk automatically closed, as he pulled off.

In a matter of seconds, they were in front of her condo.

"I'm going to need a vacation after this month is over. They got a bitch working hard. I got a portfolio, magazine photo shoot, and three hosting engagements. I'm going to need a few days off, just me, you, and the love of my life." Maxine grabbed his dick, quickly realizing he was still hard.

"You need some more? Come upstairs and spend the night, I'll cook."

"I'm flattered, but I have a test to study for, and I need to check the stock market. Maybe next week."

"When Thursday? I'm always going to be your Thursday fuck," she spat with much sarcasm.

"Look, I came home to a couple thousand after spending ten years in prison. You know first-hand, how much I had before that lady divorced me, and took everything. You grinding right?"

"I'm just..."

"No, you grinding right? You getting your money right?"

"Yeah, I'm doing okay."

"Well I'm not. Nowhere near what my hands are called for. So, we can see each other every Thursday and every other weekend or just every other weekend."

Maxine crossed her arms like a little kid. "You ain't shit. She made you evil, everybody's not like her. I know you might question me, because well you know why. But I promise you, before it's all over, you'll see my worth. Thanks for the bag, see you Thursday." She exited the car storming inside her apartment building.

****

The heat blasted as Kareem, navigated through traffic listening to *'Yo Gotti's Lifestyle'*. He couldn't phantom the thought of how he ended up dealing with another crazy ass Dominican. Don't get it fucked up, the pussy was great, and that sweet mouth was even better, the experiences was topped with the fact that she always wanted to fuck in public.

The last time they fucked in public, she'd begged him to come with her to a Beyoncé concert. While Beyoncé performed her sexual song 'ROCKET'. Maxine, slid her freak'em dress up and sat on his dick. She rode him right there from the back as if she was giving him a lap dance, moving her hips simultaneously to the moans of Beyoncé's lips. Kareem, wasn't sure if it was his dick or Beyoncé that had her cumming back to back.

As he pulled up in front of his loft, he saw his right-hand man Terrance pacing back and forth, smoking a cigarette. A sense of worry kicked in as Kareem parked and jumped out.

"What up fool, why you looking like that? Something happen to my godson, what happened?" Kareem fired.

"What up, bruh? Nah your godson's good. I just need to talk to you. I need your help, you get my text?"

"Nah, I didn't get it, hold up." Kareem, walked back to the car and retrieved his phone from the trunk. He'd learned the hard way about leaving his phone out and unlocked around Maxine. He bypassed all the missed calls and texts in search of the one from Terrance.

It read...//: *Bruh I need to borrow $750 until I get paid next week. Moni trippin' 'bout my half of the bills.*

Kareem, shook his head and looked up at his right-hand man. Sometimes, it seemed like the ten years they spent in prison had mentally and spiritually broke Terrance. Before the FEDS came, they were up seven hundred, eighty thousand dollars in cash, had a liquor store, and multiple properties they'd purchased through their Real-Estate Investment Team, they'd built with Kareem's ex-wife Vivian.

Kareem's hunger to hustle along with Terrance's thirst for gunplay, earned them a solid spot in the drug trade back home in their old neighborhood in New Jersey. Due to the new crack law and the two-point reduction for all drug cases, their twenty-five-year sentence was reduced tremendously. It was Kareem's idea to move to Salt Lake City, Utah, and start over.

He was livid when Terrance decided to bring Moni's greasy ass out here with them. Not only did she leave him after the first two years and have a baby with the opposition, she conspired with Vivian in liquidating all their properties. Her dumb ass only got fifty thousand and the liquor store which she couldn't maintain.

Vivian on the other hand, got off with three point-six million, granted half of it was rightfully hers. She was the real estate broker, who had a few properties before they met.

Her grind was what attracted him to her. Being four, years his senior he thought he had his old head. When she kept complaining about getting married, he said fuck it. What better way to secure his bag? She was sexy, smart, and ambitious. The only flaw she had was the fact, she'd left her daughter to be raised by her grandmother.

Other than that, the three years they were married were perfect, until the FEDS came.

"Look bruh, you need to go back to school and find something you enjoy doing, so you can make a career for yourself. Working those temp jobs isn't the way a gangsta like you should be living." Kareem said, peeling off twenty-five hundred-dollar bills from his bankroll.

"Thanks, bruh, I promise I'll pay you back. I just need to shut this girl up. She keeps complainin' bout the struggle. It's like she want me back in the street. Fuck dat bruh, we blessed to be home, shit we could've still been stuck inside a level seven penitentiary, carrying knives the size of my arm." Terrance replied.

"Yeah and she'd still be with the same ops she had the baby with."

"Come on, bruh. That's a dead issue, literally."

"Say less."

"About that school shit, it's not for me. I'm the type that like to get my hands dirty. You know the shit no one likes to do. Anyway, my job is making me permanent, so benefits and all 'bout to kick in. Now my baby girl can get medical care."

"Your baby girl?"

"Come on, bruh, I told you that's my daughter now. She calls me daddy, I'm the only father she knows."

"It's your world, I'm just here for you, and my godson. Moni and that lil' girl is all on you. I still don't understand how you can forgive her for all the shit she done."

"I love her bruh, stop judging me. That's my bitch. Here bruh since you only here for ya godson, take ya money back. I don't judge you for messing with ya lil' shorty. You thirty-six, running around with a what twenty-two-year old?"

"Nah she twenty-five, but you right. You're my brother so keep the money. I'll feel disrespected if you give it back. I'll just say this. You deserve better…we deserve better."

Chapter Two

Music blasted from the *'Beats by Dre'* Bluetooth, pill speaker. Moni, stomped her feet from room to room, with her ear glued to the phone. Jem wobbled around the end table, trying to dance, and walk at the same time. Her pamper reeked with a potent smell. Lil' Terrance ignored them both, with his eyes glued to the T.V. as he played his PlayStation 4, compliments of his Godfather Kareem. Terrance, entered the apartment and was instantly disgusted.

The apartment was a mess, dirty dishes, toys, and long strands of left over quick weave covered the kitchen table.

"Moni, what you do all day? Why does the apartment look like this?" Terrance fussed.

Moni, entered the living room, hair neat, face on fleek, dressed in a Burberry mini skirt, with a white Armani blouse. She looked like a Catholic school girl. Her rich dark skin complexion was what drove him crazy. Born in St. Thomas her exotic features only added to her beauty.

"Hold on Shanae, let me call you back, someone wanna come home questioning what I do all day. When I'm the only one with a real job around here." She hung up the phone and twisted her face up at Terrance.

Since he'd been home on this scared and squared shit she'd lost all respect for the once feared killer.

"What you lookin' at me like that for and why the house look and smell like this?" Terrance repeated.

"The house look like this because, one I just got in from work and had to do my client's hair. If you got me a shop like you promised, I wouldn't have to do hair in the kitchen. Two your lazy ass son been home from school and didn't do his chores, or homework. He just ran in there and picked up that game. I should break that junk."

Lil' Terrance looked at his mother, then his father for help.

"You not takin' his game." Terrance said.

"Whatever. That smell is probably your daughter, I didn't have money to get the pampers till I did my client's hair. Now that you're home I can go get some while you and your son clean up. I mean it ain't like you do nothin' else around here.

That bullshit job you got don't help none, all the bills still backed up. If I knew it was goin' to be like this. I wouldn't have come to these mountains. I could struggle back home, at least my family could've help us." Moni, nagged with a mean scowl on her face.

"I'm your family, we your fucking family. I told you I was going to get the money." Terrance pulled out the twenty-five hundred dollars, he'd got from Kareem.

Moni, smiled and greedily walked over. He counted out eight-hundred for the rent and another two-hundred for groceries.

"My car insurance due and Jem's day care bill is overdue. That's like another five-hundred, plus I need gas, and lunch money until I get paid." Moni, continued plucking bill after bill out of his hands.

"Where you get this money from, Kareem? How he still got all this money left? Y'all blaming everything on me and Viv. But, you don't wonder how he's riding around in BMWs, while you broke working odd jobs?"

"Nah I don't wonder how he up, I know. He wasn't stupid like me and trusted his girl, wife, and baby mother with everything he had. He had a lot of money invested in the stock market. So, stop with the jealous shit. Y'all both getting on my nerves. Come on, Lil' Tee turn off that game, and let's clean up."

Moni stood there with a stupid look on her face. "Lil' Terrance come and get these pampers for your sister when I ring the doorbell." she told her son.

"Daddy now that you got some money can you buy me some new Jordan's? I ain't have no new sneakers in a long time." Lil' Tee asked his father.

Terrance stared at the five-hundred-dollar bills in his hand. "I'll take you and your sister to buy some new sneakers tomorrow."

Terrance cleaned up, cooked dinner, helped Lil' Tee with his homework, then fed, burped, and rocked Jem to sleep. He placed the baby in her crib after she fell asleep on his chest. Then exited the bedroom expecting to find Moni in the living room watching a *Love & Hip-Hop* reality series marathon. Only to find the front room empty and her car keys gone. He turned on the video game awaiting her return with twenty-one questions.

****

At the University of Utah, downtown Salt Lake City. The energy in the classroom could be defined by the lackluster look on everyone's faces. Professor Al-Rekadi, completed her lecture on the differences between a CPI and a PPI. It was no surprise only one student was paying attention.

"Mr. Davis can you tell me the definition of CPI and PPI, also explain the difference?"

"C.P.I. stands for consumer price index which is the market basket of good priced at a certain level for you and I. Whereas, P.P.I. which stands for a Producer Priced Index operates from a wholesaler's standpoint." answered Kareem.

"Great job at least someone's paying attention." she praised.

Kareem couldn't understand how all the men in class didn't pay attention. Professor Al-Rekadi, was the perfect description of what a Persian goddess looked like. She stood a bit over five-feet, with almond shaped eyes, thick eyebrows, and naturally long eyelashes, that caused her to bat her eyes in a sexy calling gesture, when giving eye contact for a long time.

Just as she was doing to Kareem, now. He responded by seductively biting his bottom lip, eyeing her from top to bottom, fantasizing about relieving her handful sized breasts and wide hips from the clutches of the Saint Laurent dress suit. As he purposely focused on her beautiful toes, peeking out of her Jimmy Choo shoes, Kareem wanted desperately to suck her toes.

Professor Al-Rekadi, shied away from his eye contact. She fanned herself with the test results in her hand, shook her head, and smiled. For the past three months, they'd been playing this harmless flirting game. As a married forty-two-year old, it felt great to feel wanted.

"Alright test results are in. You'll need at least eighty percent or better, to even think about taking the Series seven or sixty-three test to become a stock broker.

As you know the test is six hours long and over two-hundred questions. If you don't stay awake or alert in my class, it will be virtually impossible for you to focus on the test." She nudged the arm of the young lady sleeping on her desk.

"I'm sorry professor Al-Rekadi, I had to work fourteen hours straight before I got here. These night classes are killing me." The young lady explained as her voice dragged with exhaustion.

"We all have responsibilities, I work sixteen hours, four days a week, every week. Yet I still, find a way to come here and put in my required four hours. It's life Ms. Flood."

As she passed out the test results, Kareem couldn't help but notice the look of despair on some of his classmates faces. He started to question his scores until he noticed, she placed his test facedown. Kareem turned the paper over to find a ninety-two percent with, *'Extra credit after class'* at the top.

As each classmate gathered their belongings, Kareem slowly placed each book inside his MCM backpack. When all the students were gone, Professor Al-Rekadi, slipped out of her heels and hopped onto the desk.

"So, you think you're ready?" She asked, looking directly into his eyes.

"Yes, ma'am, I've been studying and paying close attention. You said we had to have at least an eighty, I scored a ninety-two." Kareem proudly boasted.

"Okay, enough with the ma'am. Please call me Laylah, I know you pay attention. I personally make it my business to see that you do. Yet, I wasn't speaking on the test in that regards. I know you'll pass with flying colors. I'm asking if you're ready to stop playing this cat and mouse game and tell me what you really want?" Laylah crossed her legs exposing so much of her butter pecan thighs his dick grew stiff.

Caught off guard by her candor, Kareem swallowed a big knot in his throat, rubbed his rich dark beard, and cracked a grin.

"Well I'm not much of the talking type." Kareem said, maneuvering around the desk onto his feet. After closing and locking the door, he walked over to Laylah.

"I've always wondered what you'd look like with your hair down." He removed her hair pins, allowing her curly locks to drop down her back.

Laylah grabbed his Hermes belt buckle, while simultaneously, opening her legs, placing the heel of her feet on his ass cheeks, and forcing him closer.

Kareem ran his strong hands through her hair, palming the back of her small head. He tugged her hair enough to tilt her head and run his thick, warm tongue up the side of her neck. He nibbled on her earlobe, as saliva darkened the complexion of the small hairs running up her neck to the back of her ear.

Her hands found their way to his prize, she began stroking his length, rubbing her thumb across the smooth circumcised dick she was unaccustomed to.

Kareem closed his eyes, as she used both hands to stroke his dick. Her touch was soft and cold, the more she flicked her thumb around the head of his dick the harder he got. He removed her top, devouring her left breast. Her body was in immaculate shape for her age. Kareem rubbed his teeth against her cough drop sized nipples, causing her to moan words in her native tongue.

Laylah slipped her soft hands up his shirt, getting turned on by the definition in his chest. As she explored his arms and back, he reached into his pants pocket retrieving a condom. Laylah gave him a shove, causing him to stumble.

As she stared into his eyes, she slipped her panties off, hiked up her dress, spun around, and did a split on the desk. She leaned forward, causing her ass to toot up in the air seductively.

Kareem was shocked by her flexibility, unbeknown to him the ex-gymnast had plenty more moves. He marveled at the sight of her fat swollen pussy, to his surprise it was shaved bald. He dipped down to his knees and jammed his tongue deep inside, almost causing her to cum on spot.

"Oh my gosh, Kareem, yesss…baby just like that." She moaned.

Kareem placed his middle finger inside her pussy while he switched between lightly sucking and tongue kissing her clitoris.

"Yes…oh my gosh…Kareem baby that feels…that's it…yesss!" Laylah cried.

Laylah was so caught up in the pleasure, she spread her ass cheeks to give him more access. Kareem had a better idea, as he slid his thick long fingers in and out of her dripping, wet pussy, and licked the outside of her asshole.

"Oh no…ummm wait…I can't…breathe…what are you…please." She panted.

The double pleasure made her dizzy, causing her to lose her breath. Kareem ignored her cries, forcing his thick tongue in and out of her asshole, while using both two fingers stroking her pussy at the same fast pace. He slowed down, slid his tongue out only to suck on her swollen clit. He took it in his mouth, gently pulling on it, sucking while licking furiously in figure eight motion.

"I'm cumming…I'm cumming!" Laylah moaned, as her stomach started to quiver. Yess…Kareem." She screamed, covering her mouth with her hands, trying to muffle her cries.

Kareem continued licking and sucking on her clitoris, as her juices flowed all over his fingers and mouth. He devilishly placed one finger in her ass, two in her pussy, and his mouth on her pearl, masterfully playing her body like an instrument.

"Oh, shit no! Wait…what…oooh…what are you. Damn Kareem, please. What are you trying to do to me?" she whined, having multiple orgasms.

Kareem stood up satisfied, his dick was so hard it felt numb. He pulled Laylah to her knees and directed his long, rock-hard dick into her cum soaked pussy. She was so tight and wet the condom felt nonexistent. He reached back and pushed on his abs, trying to control his plunge.

"Oh…wait…Kareem hold up…you're so big. I can't…I can't…wait…." she pleaded as Kareem tried to ease up circling inch by inch to let her adjust to his length and size.

As Laylah started rotating her hips, meeting his slow strokes, Kareem gripped her hips, making wide circles, stroking wall to wall. He picked up the pace, grinding into her gushing canal, faster and faster.

"Yes baby…give it to me…oooh shit…you in my st…stomach…damn." She panted.

Kareem gripped her shoulders with one hand and gently but firmly placed his other hand around her throat. Then lifted her torso up, grinding his long, thick dick deep inside her.

"No…wait…Kareem. It…I can't, hold up…damnnn!" Laylah cried feeling overwhelmed by the pleasurable pain, she'd never in all of her forty-two years had her pussy filled to such capacity.

"Shhh...somebody might hear us." Kareem whispered.

"I can't Kareem your all...the...way...in meee!" Laylah whined.

"Come on now, you're a big girl, take this dick!" He demanded.

"I can't...I can't." She panted.

He pulled all the way out, then went back in using short strong strokes. "I thought you was ready, isn't this what you wanted?" Kareem teased.

"Yes...no...yes I can't...I...I..." she stuttered. "Ooh...my...gawddd!" She screamed, as he thrusted back deep into her with his long dick.

Kareem quickly placed his hand over her mouth without losing his stride.

"Ummm...ummm...ummm." The sounds of her muffled screams could be heard lightly through his strong hands.

"Aah...shit." Kareem hissed, as Laylah sinked her teeth into his finger. He paced his strokes trying to give her a reprieve, as she adjusted to his rhythm.

Laylah began throwing her perfectly round ass back at him. The sounds of her ass cheeks bouncing off his abs echoed throughout the classroom.

Kareem removed his hands from her mouth. "That's right baby throw that sexy ass back on me." Kareem encouraged, pounding away in her soaking pussy.

Matching him thrust for thrust, Laylah looked back at Kareem, feeling emboldened and sexy by the pleasure on his face, causing her to engage in his sexual banter. "Like this?" She purred, contracting her pussy muscles on his length.

"Aah shit, damn ma just like that. Damn, Laylah gimme this pussy."

"Oh, Kareem, you feel so good in me. Oh yesss!"

"Shit Laylah…this pussy so wet and tight."

"O…ohhh baby you did this to meee…you feel so good." With each wave of Kareem's strokes Laylah moaned, becoming louder with each word. "I can feel all of you Kareem, you hitting my spot. Kareem, I think I'm 'bout to cummm!" She whined.

"That's right cum for me baby, cum all on this dick." He ordered feeling his own orgasm coming on strong.

"Ohhh, I…I'm cumming. K…K…Kareem, I'm cumminggg!" Laylah exploded all over him as he'd requested.

"Damn." They said in unison.

After forty-five minutes of mind blowing sex Laylah and Kareem got themselves together and vacated the college premises.

"You make sure you study for the test, if you need any more extra credit, I'm free on Tuesdays." Laylah advised.

"Is that an indication that we can spend time together every Tuesday?" Kareem replied, licking his lips.

"Do you need extra credit?" She flirted.

"What do you think? I'm just not trying to get too attached. You are married, right?"

"You let me worry about my marriage. Besides I'm sure someone of your talents has somebody special."

"Actually, I don't, you know my story. I just came home from prison, which I'm sure you know because of all my credits that were transferred. I'm just dating nothing too serious, still finding out what I like and don't like, you know?" Kareem lightly shrugged.

"Take your time, trust me you don't want to end up stuck in a relationship you really don't want to be in." Laylah shook her head thinking about her own situation, hitting the alarm on her Lamborghini Urus.

Kareem opened her door, helping her into her SUV, admiring her taste in automobiles.

"You have a blessed night, drive safely."

"Make sure you have your assignment complete. Mr. Davis, what is the first goal of investment and why do we invest?" She transformed back into her Professor role.

"The first and main goal of investing is to beat the rate of inflation. The reason why we invest, is to look for numbers that's conducive to our lifestyle. It all depends on your personal means, as well as long term goals." Kareem proudly explain, smiling from ear to ear.

"Yes, I'm sure you'll make me a proud teacher." Laylah nodded impressed.

"Maybe at our next extra credit session, the teacher can become the student." Kareem smirked lustfully.

"I'm afraid that already happened, you have a nice night. Don't hang out too late, you will need your rest."

"Yes, Lay…I mean Professor Al- Rekadi."

"Please be careful Kareem." She stated, staring at him cautiously. "I have to get home." She said, picking up her ringing phone.

"No Problem." Kareem stepped away and walked to his coupe.

Chapter Three

I love my baby mother I'll never let her go...

The wind whistled through the cold night air like the tunes of Old Western films. Terrance, stalked his prey from fifteen feet away. The traffic flooded State Street giving him the opportunity to blend in without being noticed. Back home in New Jersey low leveled drug dealers trapped out of corner stores and bodegas. Here in Salt Lake City, they hustled in front of taco stands. After coming home last night and finding the electricity off, Terrance became furious.

His pride wouldn't allow him to ask Kareem for money again. The twenty-five hundred dollars he'd given him should have been enough. Plus, he'd been working hard bringing home almost one-thousand dollars every two weeks. Yet somehow, Moni neglected to pay the bills. Now he had to resort back to his old ways for the sake of their family.

He watched the hustler in grey jogging pants serve customer after customer. Terrance figured he must've had the best product or be the boss, because two out of three customers bought off of him. The hustler in grey jogging pants, shook hands with his cronies, while throwing up gang signs. Terrance chuckled at the sight knowing gangs were literally in every city in the country.

When he finally walked off, Terrance followed. His prey spoke on the phone oblivious to the danger lurking. As they cross each intersection Terrance closed in. He prayed the young dealer wouldn't slip into one of the many buildings before he could get in arms reach.

The young dealer stopped in front of a high-rise and looked up toward the windows. Terrance squatted down as if he was tying his shoes. A young lady threw a set of keys out the window. The young dealer picked them up off the ground, hung up his phone, and proceeded to open the front door. Terrance, came behind him, raising the gun, smacking him in the back of the head.

"Aahhh shit, what the fuck?" The young man turned around only to find the nose of a gun in his face.

"Don't scream, cry, move or even breathe. Just give me all your money and you'll live another day." Terrance ordered.

The young man could tell by his accent, he wasn't from around there. Plus, the look in his eyes said he was serious.

"Here man, please don't kill me." The young dealer struggled to pull the knot of money out of his tight pocket.

Terrance got annoyed and ripped the whole pocket off with the cash. "Give me the watch, chain, and phone."

"Not my phone man please, I need my phone."

Terrance, smacked him again with the gun. "You ready to die for that phone, huh?" He placed the gun to his head.

The young dealer tremored, before wetting his pants. Terrance desperately wanted to add another body to his resume. Then he realized if he fired the Governor inside this hallway, the whole building would hear it. He stuffed the jewelry and phone in his pocket along with the money and exited the building. Feeling like an addict who'd just relapsed, he loved the high.

****

Meanwhile...

Moni, found herself the center of attention, inside a cabin in the mountains in Ogden, Utah. The smell of liquor and weed filled the air. Cocaine covered the dining table, as heavy metal crept through the air waves. The one room cabin looked like a scene out of a horror movie. It had stone walls, pots hanging from the ceiling, wired frame furniture, and a moose head hanging over the lit fireplace. Two white men still dressed in snowboarding head gear, were enjoying her wet mouth as she took turns pleasing their pink cocks.

She slurped louder with every lick. Sucking dick turned her on. So, having one dick in her mouth and another hard dick in her hand, had her pussy soaking wet. She deep-throated his whole cock until her lips kissed his pubic hairs.

"Fuck, aahh, fuck. Yes, suck this cock!" Moni continued performing, jerking the shaft of his thick vein dick, while sucking on his fat mushroom head.

'Sluurp...slluurp... sluurp...slaaack' went the sound of her wet work.

"Aah fuck, shit my fucking coooock!" He screamed, splashing cum all over her pretty brown face.

With no hesitation she ferociously attacked the other dick like a crazed animal. She sucked the side of his long thin shaft with cum dripping down her face. Moni stood up and pushed him down onto the bed, ready to fuck. The goofy look on his face only infuriated her desire to fuck the shit out of him. She straddled his body, rocked her hips from side to side, then slammed down on his dick.

"Oh, shit." He yelled.

"Unh…unh you ever been fucked by a black woman?" Moni, taunted.

He was so caught in the pleasure, trying to keep in sync with her, rhythm, he didn't answer.

Moni smacked him across the face. "Answer me, when I'm talking to you. Have you ever been fucked by a black woman?" He shook his head. Moni smacked him again. "I said answer me, use that lil' pink mouth of yours." She ordered.

"No, no." He answered, holding the side of his face with one hand, clutching her waist with the other, trying to hang on for the ride.

Moni started twerkin' on his dick, hard and fast, each ass cheek slapping against his thighs. His partner stood behind them, staring in amazement at the way her ass cheeks opened and closed as it went up and down.

"What you doing standing around with your dick in your hand for? Come put that fat white shit in my ass." She ordered looking back at his brother.

Greg mounted her from behind, sliding his cock in her slippery wet asshole. She made her cheeks jump, one at a time, tightening her pussy and anal muscles at the same time.

She fucked the shit out of them, giving them the time of their lives for the five grand they'd paid. Unbeknown to Terrance, she'd been an escort for the last month or so. With him refusing to hustle she felt the need to take matters into her own hands. Well that was the excuse she told herself. She really just wanted to be a slut, now she was getting paid for it.

****

Kareem, scratched his head. He'd been there for almost four hours. The test was way more complicated than he thought. He'd been studying and dealing with the stock market for over fifteen years. Yet some of those questions he'd never seen before. He thought about Laylah and how disappointed she'd be if he failed. His mind drifted off to all the weekly sexcapades they'd shared.

She quizzed him by removing a piece of clothing for every answer he got correct. He remembered this question, it got her out of them red lace panties last week.

"What is the discounted value of the stream of dividends, that can be shown to produce a very simple formula for the long-run total return for either the individual stock or the market as a whole." She asked.

"Long-run equity return equals, Initial dividend, plus growth rate." Kareem smirked at the thought of her pretty ass giving him a belly dance while peeling off those red panties.

He quickly snapped out of his daze and answered the question. He regained focus and concentrated like his future depended on it.

Maxine sat behind the wheel of her new Ferrari 812 Superfast. Life had been treating her great these last few years. She'd become an overnight social media star by posting pictures, which led to numerous modeling gigs.

Her agent had just informed her, she'd be starring in a new, Tyler Perry, movie this summer. Now all she needed was for, Kareem, to stop dragging his feet and make their relationship official. Having him as her man would make her life perfect.

She pulled up in front of his loft. If this weekend didn't change his perception of her. Then she'd have to start looking elsewhere for a man to share her life with. She cracked the cheesiest smile at the sight of him standing out front. He was draped in a royal blue shearling, clutching a duffle bag, looking like a GQ model.

"Damn this man got my pussy wet." She whispered.

Kareem entered the foreign. "Damn baby I'm so proud of you. You know that?"

"Thanks babe that means a lot coming from you." Maxine blushed.

"Don't go blowing all your money. I told you the stock market is booming right now. It's cool to buy nice things but even cooler and safer to invest."

"I know, I know. Please don't ruin our trip with all them daddy lectures. You know how creepy that makes me feel. You're already an old man." She teased.

"Yeah, the coolest old man you know," He placed his bag between his legs and pulled out his phone, logging onto *E*TRADE*.

"So how did you do on your test?"

"I did all right, I think I passed."

"You passed, I got me a smart ex-gangsta."

"Did you pick up the Investment Business Daily?"

"Yes, Wolf of Wall Street." Maxine started getting upset.

Kareem, turned in her direction, feeling the vibe change. "Your hair looks nice. Jet black looks good on you. Does, that mean you're not going to be my freaky lil' blonde stripper this weekend?" He gave her a kiss on the cheek.

Maxine smiled, "You're a jerk. Why you just saying something? I'm a freak by nature. Even if I didn't have any hair, I'd still be whatever you want. Wait till we get to Vegas, I got something for you." She pulled off, shaking her head.

****

Two Months Later...

Moni rested her head on her man's lap, as he fed her strawberries dipped in chocolate. His, new found wealth ignited long, missed feelings of being safe, protected, and cared for.

As they relaxed in the comfort of their new home watching, Game of Thrones on Netflix. She admired the decor, Terrance had allowed her to decorate. Excited to indulge in her past time dream of becoming an interior decorator, she slayed the task. The living room was decorated with a caramel set, along with caramel and brown suede throw pillows.

She added matching lamps on expensive Oakwood living room tables, over dark brown carpeting. The walls were adorned with black and white paintings she got from a trendy little art shop in downtown Salt Lake City.

It was times like these that made her want to quit her night job. Especially since she only had one client she actually enjoyed spending time with. Lil' Terrance and Jem were spending the night with Shanae. Moni, was so grateful to have a friend like her. From the time they'd met at her day job, they clicked. Since Moni didn't know a soul in the foreign place they became the best of friends.

Shanae having no kids of her own fell in love with Jem, proclaiming herself as Jem's *'godmother'*. She also introduced Moni to her *'Night Job'* after listening to her complain about bills and struggling.

Terrance purposely made his dick jump against Moni's head.

"You trying to be fresh?" she questioned, in her best Rihanna impersonation.

Terrance bent over giving her a wet, sloppy kiss. Their tongues spared with the passion they once shared.

"You know, I love you, right?" He questioned, staring into her eyes.

"You know, I love you, more?" She lied, without blinking.

Terrance kissed her passionately, while ripping her purple boy-shorts panties off. Moni gushed as her ruined panties hit the floor. The one thing she loved more than sucking dick, was being manhandled. Terrance standing six-one, weighing two hundred, twenty-five pounds of solid muscles, accomplished that with ease.

Terrance placed his huge hands around her neck, forcing her from his lap. He planted a hard kiss on her soft lips, then bit down on her bottom lip causing blood to appear.

"Ouch!" Moni cried.

"Shut up." Terrance growled, standing to his feet, towering over her. His long, curvy, thick dick attempted to bust out of his basketball shorts.

Moni leaned forward and planted kisses where her name was tatted across his six-pack. She rubbed her face on his dick through his shorts. Then she licked up the middle of his stomach, from his belly button, until she was face to face with his bulging chest. She sucked on his nipple, and sunk her teeth into it, playfully paying him back.

Terrance closed his eyes tightly masking the pain. He swept her up in both hands. She grabbed the back of his nappy fro-hawk. As he cupped her ass with one hand, he used the other to release his dick. Before it could feel a touch of cool air, he forced it deep inside her dripping wet box.

"Oooh, yessss." Moni squeezed two fists full of his hair and slammed down on his thickness.

Each inch filled the insides of her pussy. Terrance grabbed both of her ass cheeks, bent his knees, and bounced her up and down while angling all eleven inches of his hooked dick at her walls. He punished her insides with each plunge, she cried in her imitation Baja accent.

"Oooh me sorry Rude boy, me sooo sorry."

"Shut up, this what you want, right?" He lifted her up before effortlessly slamming her back down on his steel-hard hook.

"Ouch, Rude boy, baby me so sorry, no. Yesss! No. I mean Yesss...I love this Rude boy dick." Moni panted, screwing up her face, while grinding into his thrusts.

"Nah, fuck dat. What's his name, call him by his name." He grinded his dick inside her using all of his back muscles.

"Cap...Cap...Captain Hook. His name is Captain Hook!" She cried, holding onto him, tightly squeezing her pussy muscles hoping this tactic would stop the assault.

To her surprise he continued bouncing her up and down, making big circles inside her walls, as their pelvises slammed into each other.

"Damn, baby! I'm sorry. Whatcha girl do? I pr...pr...promise, me be good."

Terrance squat walked with her in full stride, ramming his sword in her guts, with each step.

"Oooh, T...T...Terrance." She pleaded, as her juices dripped all over his stomach, down his thighs.

Terrance forced her against the wall. In two quick moves he slipped his forearms under her thick thighs and lifted her higher in the air. Moni, held on to his fro-hawk, as she balanced her weight by wrapping her legs around his neck. Like a wild dog, Terrance sniffed her box, inhaling the wonderful scent of *Obsession* for woman mixed with the sweet sex nectar that only Moni's box could release.

Terrance, licked the inside of her treasure sliding his tongue in and out. He placed his large hand under her soft curvy buttocks using it to hold her extended in the air. Moni, leaned her back against the wall and grinded on his face, while using his hair motioning him in what direction she wanted him to lick.

Terrance reached up and wrapped his other hand around her neck. As his grip got tighter, his tongue moved faster, viciously assaulting her clitoris. He squeezed tighter causing her to lose her breath a little. She pulled on his hair harder and started cumming all over his face. Terrance let her down and motioned for her to get on her knees. Moni obeyed, putting her bare chest on the plush carpet and her ass in the air. Terrance stood there stroking his hooked monster, with her pussy juices plastered all over his face, admiring the arch in her back. He entered her from behind, slow and hard, filling her asshole with 'Captain Hook'.

"What I…I…s…yesss…damn." Moni cried in ecstasy.

"Shut up, suck on this." Terrance stepped one foot around her and forced his big toe in her mouth. She sucked on his toe, as he pounded away in her ass.

Chapter Four

Dreams Do Come True

The Vegas night air tickled, Kareem's beard as he took a sip of *French Vanilla Patron* on the balcony of his hotel room. He watched the late-night patrons scatter in each direction, trying to imagine where they were headed.

As he took in the scenery, filled with bright lights, foreign cars, and Casino's, Kareem, daydreamed of the dark days. All those years spent locked down in a cell, he had no idea he would receive his freedom while he was still young. He had already started prepping himself to be released in his late forties, by working out, and watching what he ate.

The sound of the door opening and closing, alerted him that Maxine had returned from the casino floor. His awareness picked up the noise of more than one pair of shoes tapping the floor. He twisted his face up, perplexed by what he envisioned.

Maxine was headed in his direction, with a jaw dropping female in tow. She flashed the cheesiest grin, knowing this move would surely put her at wifey status. Kareem, slid the glass door open and adjusted his eyes, wondering if the patron was playing tricks on him.

Maxine's beautiful smile beamed over the Vegas lights. "Babe, I want you to meet somebody."

A slight sense of nervousness tried to set in. Kareem, poked his chest out, and confidently kissed Maxine on the cheek, as she passed the females hand over to him.

"Babe this is, Tender…Tender, this is my baby, Kareem."

Kareem kissed the top of her hand and his dick jumped. In front of him literally stood the woman of his dreams. Back when he was in prison, he collected every picture he could find of her. His walls, locker, and bed was filled with photos of her. His dick had a mind of its own, revisiting all the nights, mornings, and afternoons he jerked off to her pictures. The centerfold she did in Phat Puffs, showed each one of her pussy lips. The whole prison system was drooling over how fat her camel toe appeared.

"How you doing, Tender, you're even more beautiful than I thought."

"Thank you. Maxine, you said he was handsome, but I didn't know you meant breathtaking." She complimented sizing Kareem up. Kareem couldn't help but blush.

Maxine caught him, but before she could get jealous, she remembered this was her idea. "Yes, Sweetie my man looks good."

She moved in closer and planted a soft kiss on his neck. Kareem, couldn't take his eyes off Tender. She smiled at him, then looked around timidly.

"Babe remember I told you I was casted for a part in the upcoming Tyler Perry movie? Well, I got the part, Tender here is playing my girl in the movie."

"Congrats…hold up, you said your girl? What like girlfriend or like girrlllfriend?"

"The latter." Tender, answered, closing in on Maxine, placing her arm around her waist.

Maxine was the one blushing now, while Kareem rubbed his thick beard wondering if they were thinking what he was thinking.

"So, listen Babe, I told Tender how much of a crush you have on her. How you had more pictures of her than me on your wall locked up." She playfully smacked him on the chest.

"Anyway, we have to build some chemistry for the film. Plus, you need to know, I'm your woman, and can make all your dreams come true. Also, this bad ass Hindu and Chinese beauty got a thing for my Dominican, butter pecan, fat ass." Maxine placed Tender's hand on her ass, forcing her to squeeze. "You don't mind sharing me, as long as you get to live out your dream, right?" Maxine flirted.

Kareem was at a loss for words, Maxine's bluntness always turned him on. It was her who ignited the start of their relationship in the first place.

"Babe if you don't grab all this ass. This not a dream. Here feel, this soft shit." Maxine gripped a handful of Tender's ass and shook it. Kareem followed her lead, his hand nearly melted into her flesh.

"Yeah, that shit soft right? Go head kiss her. I tasted those lips in the elevator. Them things sweet and soft."

Kareem shook his head looking back and forth from, Maxine to Tender, then shrugged his shoulders. Tender batted her eyes a few times. Her glare became lower than usual. Kareem knew all too well what that meant. He licked his lips before kissing her, pecking, then sucking on her bottom lip. He clutched Maxine's ass in one hand, Tender's in the other.

"Ummm." She moaned.

Kareem slid his tongue in her inviting mouth. Her tongue was small but thick. He noticed her saliva was even pleasant, as the very fragrance of her breath seduced him. Strawberries and watermelon mixed with a touch of peppermint. Maxine rubbed small circles on both their backs, as she watched Tender place both hands on his chest then push off. Her eyes were nearly shut.

"Humph, it's something about a man that knows how to kiss." She said before fully gathering her thoughts.

Maxine, refused to be out done. She began kissing Tender passionately, while grabbing Kareem's dick through his pants. Ready to show off her professional skills, she unbuckled his pants, finding the love of her life, locked, and loaded. Maxine took Tender's hand and placed it on his hard dick.

They both began stroking his length at the same time with their tiny soft hands. Kareem, slid both his hands up the back of their dresses. Not surprised that neither of them was wearing panties. He used his thumbs and pinkies to spread both of their cheeks apart. He strategically plunged his middle finger inside their warm wet pussies.

He began finger fucking them at the same pace, as they striked his long fat dick. Maxine broke away from the hold of Tenders soft lips and began kissing her man. Tender took this time to grind back on his magical fingers until she came. Maxine felt Tender's body tremble. Not wanting to let go of Kareem's dick, she used one hand to remove Tenders spaghetti strap. The firmness of her breasts, topped with the size of her areola, made her jealous. She took one in her mouth causing Tender to scream.

"Ahhh, yes. That's my spot," Maxine sucked on her nipple then devoured her areola.

"Ummmh…Mommie, that feels good." Tender closed her eyes, enjoying the skills of Maxine's warm tongue.

Kareem decided to join in. He shed her other strap and took a manly portion of her breast his mouth.

"Oh, my Goddd, damnnn, y'all about to make me cum againnn…"

Kareem used his tongue to perform circles around her nipples, while sucking on her beautiful breasts. He continued to work his magical fingers until they both came. Both women dropped to their knees, racing to feel his long thick dick in their mouths.

Maxine was the first to find the love of her life. She planted soft kisses up the side of his shaft, then licked all ten and half inches, until she greedily began sucking his dick.

Kareem placed the fingers he had in Maxine's pussy into Tender's mouth. She sucked on his finger as if it was his dick.

Looking up at him she attempted to do a better job than Maxine did on his actual dick. She licked all of Maxine's juices from his fingers and hand.

Maxine, popped his dick out of her mouth. "Here my love have a taste." Maxine, grabbed Tender's long black hair, forcing Kareem's dick in her mouth. She sat back and watched her small mouth try to deep throat her man's big long dick. Kareem placed the finger he had inside Tender's tunnel, into Maxine's mouth.

"Like how her pussy tastes?" He asked.

Maxine sucked on Kareem's finger until every scent of Tender's juices were gone. She looked up at her man, as he stood there with his eyes closed enjoying Tender's mouth. She grabbed his ass cheek and the back of Tender's head, making him fuck her mouth.

"Yeah, right there. Ummm…right there suck this dick."

Maxine started sucking on his balls causing him to explode.

"Fuck, yeah, damn." Kareem moaned.

Cum spilled out of the side of Tender's mouth. Maxine, licked the cum off the side of her face, not wanting to let a drop of his delicious cum go to waste. She jerked him off as, Tender, continued sucking his dick. Maxine, playfully pulled his dick out of her mouth and slurped at the hole of his dick. A long, spaghetti like string of cum exited his dick, disappearing down her throat. She skillfully sucked his dick, knowing just how to make it stay hard. She held his dick, concentrating on the head.

Tender, stood up not knowing how to take Maxine's actions. She felt the sense of jealousy, so she moved over towards the balcony, to watch the skyline. She wondered if anybody had been watching them. Her juices dripped down her leg, at the sound of Maxine, slurping on Kareem's long, thick, dick.

Kareem, opened his eyes, and found Tender leaning over the balcony banister. The bottom of her mini-skirt was still hiked up over her thick thighs. The sight of her heart shaped ass and luscious pussy bent over the rail gave him an idea. Maxine, had done her job, his dick was harder than ever. Kareem tugged on the back of her hair, motioning for her to release his dick. As they lock eyes, he nodded his head toward Tender.

Maxine, read his mind and was first to approach, Tender. Still in a pleasing mood, she dropped down to her knees, spread Tender's ass cheeks and licked her from her pussy to her ass hole. Tender's body jumped when, Maxine's warm, wet tongue slid in and out her ass hole. Kareem placed his Popeye, sized forearm on her lower back causing her to extend over the banister. The night air and the bright lights mixed with Maxine's skilled tongue, released her alter ego.

"Oh shit…your tongue feels so gooddd…" Tender purred.

Kareem, leaned over and licked the tip of her ass crack, down to her butt hole. He slammed his tongue inside her tunnel as Maxine tongue kissed her clitoris.

"Oohhh…ssshittt! Damn, stop please…pleassse stop. Wait…wait, I can't breathe." Tender squealed.

Kareem's dick was so hard it stood straight up. He kissed Maxine, in between licking Tender's ass hole. They tongue fought over who was going to suck her clitoris. Tender tasted so good, he could no longer resist. He guided his dick into her sweet wet pussy, on an angle, so Maxine could still taste her and him. Her tunnel was wet, but small.

"Nooo…oh noo…sss…please wait." She cried as he entered her.

"Shush, calm down, I got you." Kareem whispered.

"Okay…aahhh…owww. Yes! Yessss…go slow."

Kareem slow stroked her pussy, it was so tight he had to focus. The feeling of her drenched insides, tempted him to go deeper. He needed to feel all of her. Maxine, sucked on his balls, knowing all too well how it felt the first time she got fucked by that, 'Monsta.'

Kareem, winded his hips in small circular motions, while slowly sliding deeper inside her tight soaked pussy.

"Fuck…yes. Damn baby…it's big…it's big. I'm…I'm ready." She panted.

Kareem stepped over Maxine, who sat on the ground underneath them. As he stretched out Tender's insides, Maxine, licked from her clit to Kareem's balls. Tender began to get dizzy. She wasn't sure if it was from Kareem's huge dick or from her hanging upside down over the banister, holding on for dear life.

To add more excitement, Kareem, snatched her legs from under her. He tossed her up and over the banister, until he had a vice grip on her ankles. Tender was beyond afraid, her long breasts jiggled in the air, as Kareem's long, slow strokes never seemed to end. He held her in a wheel barrel position, causing her to meet his thrust forcefully.

"Yes…yes, right there…damn I'm…I'm…I'm cumming!" Tender moans grew louder. Being suspended in midair, getting long dicked by Kareem, gave her the strongest orgasm she'd ever had.

"Daddy I want to please you," she whined as her body.

Kareem released her ankles and allowed her to get in position.

Tender eased down to his waist then slid her tongue up and down the crack of Kareem's asshole. She paid extra attention to the sensitive part between his balls and anus, before sliding back up to his balls sucking, slobbering and humming on them.

As he began to get weak she placed her finger on his taint applying a little pressure, while licking his asshole.

"Oh shit, damn girl. What you doing…fuck." Kareem, grunted as he pulled out and exploded all over Tender's big round ass.

He let go of her ankles, so she could come from over the bar. Tender slid down to the ground, her body was exhausted.

"Alright, now Mama. it's my turn. I picked up some glow in the dark body paint. We about to make an X-rated Picasso." Maxine stated.

She helped Tender up, then she and Kareem, carried her to the bedroom.

Chapter Five

Pretty Lil' Liar

The air conditioner pumped out ice cold air, as the scent of different body odors filled the room. Terrance placed the dumbbells down and lowered the volume on his iPad. Working out seemed to be the safest way to relieve stress. Lately, for reasons unknown to him, Moni, was never home. His job had been cutting his hours every week and his trigger finger had been whispering to him daily. He'd been pulling off a few licks to stay afloat, but his real passion was murder. However, because of Lil' Terrance and Jem, he didn't want to resort to his old ways. After he felt tight and pumped he grabbed his towel.

"Excuse me, ladies." He said passing a group of women on his way into the showers.

"No, excuse us." Heather eyes grew staring at the bulge in his sweatpants. Her friend Lisa couldn't help but lick her lips.

Terrance cracked a smile and continued diddy bopping to the shower. After a long shower he decided to relax in the steam room. To his surprise he found the same two women, also enjoying the steam room. Clad with just his towel around his waist, he confidently strolled in and sat down directly across from them.

They begin whispering and giggling, as they openly admired his chiseled physique and healthy dick print. Terrance couldn't help noticing how beautiful and sexy they were.

"So, what's the funny secret?" He quizzed.

"Oh, I apologize on behalf of me and my friend we were just being silly. My name is Lisa, this is Heather."

"Oh yeah, well Lisa, Heather, I'm Terrance. I still want to know what's so funny."

Heather blushed, covering her eyes, Lisa, clawed each hand from her face. Heather still didn't look in Terrance's direction.

"I know this is Utah and all, but I'm sure, I'm not the first black man she's seen."

"No, she just can't keep her eyes off of that." Lisa pointed at his crotch.

"What this?" Terrance said, grabbing a fist full of dick, biting his bottom lip.

Heather, squeezed her legs closed, as she watched him massage his dick. It grew bigger with every motion. Lisa didn't realize her own reaction, until her fingers touched the moisture between her legs. Terrance cracked a smile realizing he had them both totally captivated.

A fat elderly white woman, entered the steam room. They all quickly paused from touching themselves. The lady smiled at the two girls but ignored Terrance.

Heather was first to notice her ignorance and rolled her eyes. Then looked back in Terrance's direction, his dark smooth skin, strong facial features, and amazing build, reminded her that she'd never been with a black man.

Terrance picked up on the elderly lady's vibe and stood to exit. "You ladies enjoy the rest of your evening."

"You too." Lisa responded.

Heather never really noticed the exchange, because she was still staring at his print. She shook her head, admiring the misty water dripping down his chiseled torso. Her pussy leaked as she watched him walk away. The muscles in his legs and rear, poked out of the towel. Heather felt like part of her soul was leaving, so, she jumped up and ran after, Terrance. Lisa had no choice, but to chase after her friend.

"Terrance, can you please hold up?" Heather requested.

Terrance turned around to find Heather's green eyes sizing him up. "What's up?"

"Some people are just stupid. I would curse her out, but she's probably old enough to be my mother."

"Yeah, it's cool, been through that a lot since I've been out here."

"Where are you from? You sound like you're from the East Coast somewhere?"

"New Jersey." Terrance proudly responded.

Lisa enveloped her arm around Heather. "Well me and my friend, was wondering if we could take you out? You know show you how hospitable we are in Utah. You ever been to a Rave?"

"Nah, can't say that I have." Terrance couldn't laugh.

These young girls had no idea how old he was. He thought about Kareem and his young girl. These two didn't look a day over twenty-five.

"Well let's exchange numbers so we can meet this weekend." Lisa boldly suggested.

After getting dressed they met at the juice bar for drinks, small talk, and to exchange numbers. Terrance's heart would always be with Moni, but she was never around anymore. It was for that reason alone, he'd planted a tracking device on her car.

****

Park City, Utah…

Moni attempted to unwind across the top of a California king size pillow top mattress. She loved when her favorite client called. The luxury cabin resembled a home from the Lifestyle of the Rich and Famous. Reza, made sure the home was decorated with all the similarities of a Middle Eastern castle.

The corridors were dressed in large gold elephant statues. Elegant rich Persian rugs draped the walls. Every piece of furniture was purchased without regards of the price, down to the gold silverware. The driveway was flooded with every Mercedes-Benz from the G-Wagon to the S-Class. Once a month she spent a whole day with him.

All the arguing and fighting, Terrance, did with her would not keep her from this experience. Reza, not only paid well, he also spoiled her with expensive gifts. They'd just returned to the cabin after dining at Lacai. The location of the five-star restaurant allowed for fine dining, while enjoying the Lakefront view. Moni's phone rang, she noticed the New Jersey area code, but not the number,

"Hello." She asked.

"What's up, gurl, how you doing?" a familiar voice asked.

"Who is this?" Moni questioned.

"It's me Moni…Vivian, don't act like you forgot my voice. I know it's been sometime, but…"

"How'd you get my number? What made you find me?" Moni cut her off, feeling uncomfortable.

"I ran into your sister, Mina, at Fridays. You know that's my girl. She said you'd moved out West with Terrance. I heard him and Kareem are home."

"Yeah, I'm out here in the mountains with Terrance. Kareem's out here, too." Moni confirmed.

Vivian didn't respond at first. Her main motive was to find Kareem, but she didn't want to sound too obvious.

"Where are y'all staying on the West Coast? I might have some time off, we need to catch up."

"Girl, knock it the fuck off, you only checking for Kareem fine ass. We out in Utah." Moni heard Reza coming up the stairs, she rushed Vivian off the phone.

"Look girl I'm going to text you Kareem's number, so you can call him. I don't want you popping up out here and end up missing him. You know what you did? Kareem's not like Terrance, I have to go."

"What you mean, what I did? You..." the phone died.

Moni hung up on Vivian, as Reza entered the room, dressed in a designer silk robe with matching boxers and slippers. Multiple gold chains rested on his hairy chest and multiple big, expensive, gold rings on his fingers.

"There's my handsome Sultan."

"Yes, I maybe your King, but you're my Little Black Nubian Queen." He said walking up beside her playing with her long box braids. "I love it when you wear your hair like this. It reminds me of what's her name? The Jackson sister..."

"Janet." Moni laughed.

"Yeah, Janet Jackson when she played in that movie with the famous rapper, you Americans are crazy about."

"Tupac is not just a rapper, but yes I got my hair done just for you. This what you like and my job is to appease you." Moni stripped down to her birthday suit, with her hand on her hip, and foot on her calf, posing in her best hood rat stance.

Reza was mesmerized by her thick shape and extra-large ass. Now his wife was beautiful and in perfect shape, but Moni's dark rich skin, wide hips, ghetto sized ass, and Janet Jackson braids drove him crazy. His infatuation for a certain type of black woman was answered when he first laid eyes on her.

"Come my King, I mean Sultan. I'm ready to be your human sex toy." Moni flirted.

Reza, grabbed the anal beads and nipple clamps out of his, 'Pleasure Chest.' He placed them down next to Moni, then grabbed the massage oil. He removed his robe, squirted oil into his short, thick hands, and rubbed them together, feeling cool quickly turn to warmth. Reza, rubbed the oil across Moni's huge behind, as she laid across the bed.

Reza was turned on by the way her fudge brown complexion glistened from the oil and lighting, he reached for the anal beads. He lubricated them with K-Y silicone oil, then slowly forced each bead into her asshole. Moni gripped the sheets tightly moaning, as the beads got bigger and bigger.

Reza rubbed her clit with his other hand, noticing some resistance after the fifth bead disappeared inside her.

"Hmm…hmm…hmm…" Moni tried to contain herself.

Reza didn't like when she talked dirty to him.

He got off by her totally submitting to his dominance. He speeds up his hand work, using the tip of his fingers, caressing her clitoris until it was swollen. Her pussy oozed, making her bite down on the pillow to stop from screaming. He added more pressure, as he stuffed the sixth bead inside her. Suddenly and swiftly, he ripped them out of her in one swift motion, while rapidly rubbing her clitoris.

"Aahhh…hmm…hmm…hmm…" she panted, trying to stay conscious.

A big glob of cum squirted out of her pussy and asshole simultaneously. Her hands lock up and began to shake as she clinched the sheet.

He turned her limp body over and found her lips quivering. "My Queen, are you alright? Did you have enough?"

Moni shook her head. The longer he got to experience with her body, the more she got paid. Reza placed a clamp on each one of her nipples. The chain extended down to her clit, where he pinched her swollen button gently, and placed the clamp on. He tugged on the center of the chain, making her nipples and clitoris stretch.

Already feeling extremely sensitive from her explosive double orgasm, Moni inhaled deeply. He took off his silk boxers, exposing his short five and half inch, thick uncircumcised dick. Moni closed her eyes, trying to control her heavy breathing. He placed the chain in between his teeth loosening the restraint. She automatically spread her legs open, after hearing him open a condom. He entered her slippery, wet box with ease, while tilting his head back to make the chain tighten.

Moni unconsciously arched her back. He pushed down, and stroked her wet pussy slowly, pulling on the chain each time he dug deeper.

"Ughhh…your…H…H…Highness." She panted, as he reached for her red g-string, stuffing them in her mouth.

The pain and pleasure from the clamps had her ready to scream. He worked his tools like a pro. His thickness filled her walls. Reza grabbed a pillow placing it under her lower back and began slowly fucking her with force. The head of his dick started hitting her G-spot. A mixture of feelings spread throughout Moni's body.

She wanted to grab him, scream, talk dirty, and kiss him passionately, while locking her legs, but she knew better. Like a good submissive woman, she bit down hard on the g-string, breathing hard through her nose. She squinted her eyes every time he tugged on the chain. She felt his dick swell, each time it banged against her G-spot, causing her to clutch the sheets even tighter. As she felt her climax building up strongly, his strokes become faster, and more powerful, each thrust harder than the last.

Reza, massaged her breasts with his hands, gripping the clamps off with his mouth, causing them both to cum hard. Afterwards, he collapsed on her, breathing heavily. Moni, passed out and they both fell into a deep slumber.

*****

Meanwhile…

Terrance sat parked outside the gated community. The tracking device he'd placed on her car, led him to this upscale neighborhood. He peeked through the gate searching for Moni's car. Locating her Benz alongside other multiple luxury vehicles. He knew she was cheating, the endless shopping

67

bags, late-night, two-hour store runs, along with the couple nights a month she didn't even come home.

"I can't believe this bitch, after all the shit she put me through." Terrance pressed speed dial on his cell, her voice service picked up.

He called her five times back to back before turning his phone off. The pain in his chest, became stronger, he could actually feel it crumbling to pieces.

Kareem's voice come to mind. *"Fuck her bro. You deserve better. She was sleeping with the opposition. Bro she conspired with that bitch Vivian to rob us."*

Terrance dialed Kareem's number, to his surprise he was sent to voicemail. He decided to drive home knowing Kareem would call back soon, plus the kids would be coming home in the morning.

Chapter Six

White Girl Wasted

AREA 51 was packed over capacity, music blasted as party goers danced to a sound foreign to Terrance's ears. Heather and Lisa, took turns grinding their small behinds on his dick. The D.J. wearing a Jig Saw mask, changed the entire mood of the club with a switch of his iPod. Everybody started jumping up and down, screaming as loud as possible. The bright lights flashed, fog came from the ceiling, as each party goer, holding a glow stick swung it in the air.

"Are you having a good time?" Heather yelled.

Terrance forced a smile, nodding his head. He was still thinking about Moni.

"Loosen up a little, here take one of these, and have a drink." Lisa placed an ecstasy pill on her tongue and slid it into his mouth. They kissed passionately, making them the center of attention. Terrance was the only black person in the whole club. Not wanting to be out done, Heather joined in.

She kissed him, then tilted Terrance's head back and poured Remy Martin XO into his mouth.

As the liquid spilled, sliding down his lips and cheeks, Heather and Lisa, sipped from his face like a water fountain.

"Wowww...I'm getting hot." Heather peeled off her top, exposing her B cups and six pack.

She then pulled Lisa's shirt over her head, causing her C's to nearly spill out of her push-up bra. They begin seducing, Terrance, by placing his hands on both of their breasts. Lisa dipped her tiny hand down the front of his pants.

"Mmmm...fuck, Heather, you have to touch his thing."

Her whole forearm disappeared as she stroked his dick, eleven inches of all meat, the hook increased her curiosity.

Heather unzipped his pants and wrestled his fat cock from Lisa's grasp. His cock hung out of the front of his boxers. Heather stroked him, squeezing his dick, making the head swell.

She whispered in his ear, "I want to taste it."

In the middle of the dance floor, she squatted in front of him, and sucked the head of his dick.

Terrance looked around, noticing that one out of eight couples were making out, or indulging in some sexual act.

Heather's pink lips covered the first five inches, slightly past the hook. Her mouth was warm, wet, and deep. Terrance's insides got warm. The lights and music intensified his high. The alcohol caused his dick to get longer each time Heather bobbed her fire red hair up and down.

Lisa, bent down to whisper something into Heather's ear. She removed his gigantic dick form the clutches of her wet strong jaws. They both seized a handful of his dick, luring him to the back of the club. Heather, flashed a big smile at every woman, who stared at Terrance and his considerable sized dick. He scanned the scenery, as women danced naked on top of speakers.

One woman strapped with a fifteen-inch dildo, pounded away at what appeared to be a midget from behind. Other women stood in line waiting to get their insides rearranged. Approaching the back of the factory, couples hung from sex swings thirty feet in the air. The foam machine went off, covering everybody on the stage in foam. They screamed louder, shaking their glow sticks, to the beat of the music.

"Come on we're going up there in one of those cages." Lisa stated.

"Why don't we join them?" Heather asked, pointing at the party of twenty engaged in an orgy.

"I'm not sharing all this with nobody, but you tonight." Lisa stroked Terrance's dick, while they waited for the man at the control booth, to bring down one of the empty cages.

"Well, we'll see what it tastes like, you're being stingy." Heather squatted and placed her thin pink lips around the head of his dick.

Her mouth was small but wetter and warmer than Lisa's. She grabbed the base of his dick, jerking him off, while sucking on the head of his swollen tip.

"Damn this shit taste good, I want you to fuck me in my ass." Heather panted.

She jerked and sucked him faster, drooling on the thickness of his dick.

Terrance caressed her face with one hand, clutching her ear, and the back of her head, as he stared into her gray eyes.

"No hands." He removed her hand from his dick and slow grinded in and out of her tiny wet mouth.

"Come on the cage is ready." Lisa ordered.

The music stopped as they entered the gate. The cage was eight feet tall, four feet wide, and three feet long. Inside sat a metal chair bolted to the floor.

Once the cage was secure, the man at the control pressed a few buttons until they were suspended fifty feet in the air. He placed them directly over the main dance floor.

Lisa and Heather shared a passionate kiss. A light breeze passed through carrying the scent of Vick's. Everybody including the girls were vaped up.

"Come on daddy thick dick, my ass needs a filler upper." Heather placed her knees in the seat of the chair, arched her back, and totted her ass in the air.

Terrance couldn't help but notice the roundness in her ass. With her being a white girl, her ass spread wide, with a nice enough cuff to lift up.

"Let me get it ready for you."

Lisa struggled with holding her balance as the cage swung back and forth. She lifted Heather's plastic mini skirt and licked the crack of her ass.

"Oooh…yes!" Heather screamed.

Lisa spread her ass cheeks and stuck her sloppy tongue in her ass hole.

"Yes…yes, oooh yes."

Terrance's dick got harder, soon as he realized Heather was a screamer. He moved Lisa out of the way. Trying to keep his balance as well, he grabbed her waist with one hand, his dick with the other. Lisa took him in her mouth magically placing a condom on. She threw the magnum wrapper down.

"Perfect fit, she's all yours." Lisa purred as she got into position.

Terrance eased his mushroom size head into her dripping wet asshole.

"Oh, God, no…gosh, it's too big. No!"

"You said you want to get fucked in the ass, right?" Terrance reminded.

Heather nodded her head. Terrance, lubricated the condom with the juices from her pussy.

"Oohhh… yes." She moaned at the feeling of his dick rubbing up and down her clit.

Terrance slowly forced the head of his dick into her anal cavity. He pulled back a little, then spit in the crack of her ass, watching it drip down her entrance.

"Aahhh, don't stop. Aahhh…yes, put that shit in my ass. Aahhh…fuck. Y…yes…ahhh. Oh, my fucking gosh it's huge. Damn it's huge!"

Terrance slow stroked her asshole, after getting the head in. Her asshole hugged the width of his dick. He speeds his strokes going deeper and deeper, realizing Heather was throwing her soft round milky ass back at him.

"Ahh…ooh…fuck me."

Her screaming turned him on, so he began to plow every inch inside her, nearly causing her to black out. The music began, and the crowd erupted, more foam and fog sprayed the entire club.

Terrance pumped away endlessly at her insides. Her body became feeble. He felt his balls boil, with no hesitation, he exploded inside her. Pumping away until every drop was in the condom, then he pulled out.

Lisa greedily removed the condom and slurped away at all the cum plastered against his dick. She remembered him cursing, Heather, out for using her hands, so she cleaned all the semen off his rock-hard dick with her tongue. Once again just like magic, she placed a condom on. They both moved Heather from the chair to the floor.

Lisa pressed her body against the cage, holding onto the bars. She arched her back then turned to Terrance, without speaking a word he snatched the Velcro from her nude color leggings.

Her pussy was hot, pink, and fat. Her lips hung out the bottom giving him a clear view. He could see the moisture dripping from her lips. Terrance pressed his weight against her back, squatting under her, wrestling his huge hooked dick,

75

inside her walls. She held onto the gate for leverage. The cage began to swing faster as he deepened his thrust.

"Give it to me." She ordered

Terrance stroked harder trying to punish her for everything Moni did. He bit down harder on his bottom lip, his hooked dick banged against melting walls, causing her to squeal.

"Smack my ass, pull my hair, treat me like the dirty slut I be."

Terrance leaned against her, grinding deeper, he placed his face to hers. "What you say?"

"Fucking spank me, treat me like a whore."

As requested, Terrance smacked her ass, leaving bruises. She invited the pain. He pulled her hair and wrapped his huge hand around her neck. She came at the touch of his grip. He squeezed tighter realizing she was like Moni. She could only reach her peek if he was ruff. He smashed her face against the cage, slamming his dick in and out of her pussy.

"Yes, fuck me. You black muthafucka. Fuck this good white, pink pussy. Call me a slut!"

"Take this dick, you slut." Terrance commanded smacking her ass. He was angry and aroused by her shit talking.

Heather regained consciousness just in time to witness the assault. She crawled to her feet and placed her small fingers against Lisa's clitoris. Her lips found hers, as Terrance aggressively pounded away.

"Fuck me...yes fuck..."

"Shut up, you slut...you white whore. You love this big fat black dick?" She shook her head yes. Terrance smacked her ass, "Answer me when I'm talking to you."

"Yes oooh...yes. I...I...love...that big fat black dick. Oh gosh, I love it...I fuckin love it."

****

Meanwhile at Kareem's Loft...

Kareem sat at his desk at the laptop, studying E Trade. He'd been here for hours, waiting for Laylah to call. She left a message saying the test scores were delivered to the school's mailroom earlier that day. She was supposed to call when she got them. That was six hours ago. The phone finally rung, Kareem answered expecting to hear Laylah's voice.

"Hello."

"Who's this, Laylah?"

"No, this isn't, Laylah. I see somebody has moved on?"

"You forgot my voice already Kay?"

77

Kareem's head started aching, his temples started pulsating. "What you want, how you get my number?"

"I want to talk to you, I want to say sorry."

"You got my money?"

"I miss you Kay, I still think about you every night."

"I think about my money every night. You got my money? What you owe us…one point eight million?"

"Kareem, I don't have the money right on. The market crashed during to recession…"

Kareem hung up the phone, it immediately started ringing again.

"Yo, stop calling my fuckin phone, unless you got my fucking money."

"Excuse me?"

"Oh, my bad Laylah. What's up?"

"What's the problem? Who owe you money? Remind me never to get on your bad side, you sound dangerous."

"It's a long story. What's up, though? How did I do?"

"So, are you serious about opening an investment club?"

"Yeah, I guess. What you saying I didn't pass? I'll only open the investment team, if we can't partner on a stock broker firm."

"Well let's get ready to open the firm."

"You serious, I passed?"

"Yes, you did great, I knew you would. Celebration on me, meet me at the airport tomorrow at nine a.m. I'm treating you to an unforgettable vacation, five days, and four nights. No phone, just us. Remember everything is on me, no tricks."

N. TROUBLE

Chapter Seven

No Good Deed Goes Unpunished

Kareem and Laylah's hired driver dropped them off at the doors of an expensive clothing optional resort on the outskirts of Cancun, called 'Desire Pearl'.

Laylah entered the lobby with Kareem in toe. An awkward feeling crept up Kareem's bones. Dozens of couples strolled around *'Nude'*, without a care in the world. Some sensed the rookie stench, Kareem's stares confirmed.

"Hey, how are you doing today buddy?" They were greeted by an uppity older fat white man as his balls sagged past the length of his pink penis.

Kareem turned to Laylah, already at the desk talking to a beautiful receptionist.

"Jacuzzi happy hour…Oh excuse me, Mrs. Al-Rekadi, I see you're a member of our exclusive club. So, you know Jacuzzi happy hours are still at six p.m., clothing is only required at restaurants, and inside the dance club, no photos, and try not to stare." She emphasized looking directly at Kareem.

"Here's a pamphlet, enjoy your stay," she handed a key card to Laylah.

"Don't tell me your shy. I told you I had a surprise. Just relax, you'll feel better once you're out of those clothes. I promise you it will be fun."

Laylah leaned in and placed a soft wet kiss on his lips, adding just enough tongue to make his dick hard. She pulled away and headed for the elevator.

Kareem shook his head. Following her to the elevator. He noticed a young man who seemed to be in his mid-twenties, long stroking a woman twice his age from behind. The elderly lady's breasts looked fresh from Dr. Miami. Her dark hair, wildly covered her face. She removed her hair looked up and waved. The young man flashed a big smile and threw up the right on sign.

Laylah and Kareem waved back and entered the elevator. When the door closed, Laylah turned and faced him.

"Please don't judge me, I am a human being with a huge sexual appetite. Like the majority of the guests here, I'm smart, rich, extremely successful, and like to have fun. Some of the couples here are swingers. I've tried that before and will leave that open for you to decide. Honestly, I'd hate to share that big black dick of yours, but I do want us to live in the moment."

"Hold up don't that swinging shit be same sex as well? I'm not wit' that shit Laylah." Kareem frowned his face, shaking his head.

The bell rang, and the elevator door opened. A Korean couple totally naked, greeted them with smiles and extended hands.

"Hi, I'm Wu, this is my wife Jeanie." He shook Kareem's hand and kissed Laylah on the cheek.

"Hi, I'm Laylah, this is my boyfriend Kareem."

Jeanie shook Laylah's hand and stood on her tippy toes, kissing Kareem on the cheek. Her breasts rubbed against him, stiffening his semi hard dick. Jeanie smiled then followed her husband inside the elevator.

"See you guys around." Wu yelled as the doors closed.

Quickly reaching their room, Laylah continued explaining how things worked in this community.

"I know you're not into any funny business. Did you pay attention to how that Korean couple greeted us? He shook your hand and kissed me.

"She shook your hand and kissed you?"

"That's how each couple signifies their interest. If they only shake hands that means each person is off limits. If the woman kisses both parties, then their open for whatever."

"So, would I be rude if I stopped them from kissing me? I mean not for nothing, but their lips could be anywhere at any time."

"Nah, you wouldn't be rude. Come on let's get undressed and do a little sightseeing before Jacuzzi happy hour starts."

****

Back in Utah...

Terrance braced himself, trying not to be heard. It was dark and cold, he'd been there over three hours. The brakes squeaked, the car came to a stop. This didn't seem like the regular traffic stop. The volume faded, followed by the window rolling down.

"It's me, Moni."

A loud buzzing sound was consolidated by what seemed to be a gate opening. The car pulled off and Terrance got excited. He'd been watching Moni's movements closely for the last couple of months. Around this time last month, he followed her to the same location he tracked her down at tonight. Once again, he found himself stuck outside the gate. Soon as she came home with long box braids, he devised up his plan. Now he laid inside the trunk of her car. He was sure to get inside the gated community now. As the car pulled over Terrance's mind wandered.

Who could she possibly be meeting in this neighborhood? Is she cheating? Where did she meet this person? Are they rich? Why didn't she leave me yet if they can afford to give her what I can't?"

"My Sultan don't you look handsome." Moni smiled.

"Ah, my Black Nubian Queen, always a pleasure to see your beautiful face." Reza greeted.

"That's the only beautiful thing about me you love to see?" Moni asked.

"Not at all doll, come on let's get you inside. Maria has prepared your favorite dish. She had a family emergency, so it will just be me and you for the whole weekend." Reza instructed.

"So, if Maria is gone who's going to wait on us?" Moni questioned.

"Guess you'll have to put on a maid outfit and spice up the weekend." Reza smirked lustfully.

"Oh, you know I'm down for anything if the price is right." Moni, replied seductively.

"You know that's never been a problem. Let me grab your bags out of the trunk." Reza stepped to the back of the car.

Terrance pulled his mask over his face and grabbed his pistol as tight as possible. Moni sounded like she was prostituting, with all the talk about doing anything for the right price. The man's accent informed him that he was from the Middle East.

The trunk opened, Reza was still talking while looking at Moni. Terrance pointed the chunky Governor directly at Reza's head.

"Don't scream, run, or move." Terrance ordered, calmly climbing out of the trunk.

"What is this? You bring your thug friend to my home to rob me? You fucking, whore!" Reza angrily spat.

Terrance slapped him across the head with the pistol. "Don't talk like that to my wife."

"B…babe, what are you doing? W…why are you in my trunk?" Moni, struggled to get the words out, fearing the worst.

"Shut up. Let's go, we're going to have ourselves a lil' talk." He placed the pistol in Reza's waist and grabbed Moni by the braids.

As they entered the cabin, Terrance, was impressed. The place was lavish. This may have been the big lick he was looking for. He quickly noticed numerous cameras all around the cabin. Each room seemed bigger than the last. He calmly walked them to the master bedroom, where he found whips, anal beads, nipple clamps, blindfolds, and numerous other toys, spread out over the huge bed.

"Looks like y'all was having a party. Too bad I had to crash it. Moni grab the blindfold and help me tie this trick ass muthafucka up." Terrance said.

"You, filthy whore, everything I did for you, and this is how you repay me?" Reza barked at Moni, anger seeping with every word.

"What did I tell you about your mouth?" Terrance barked, smacking him with the gun again.

"Fuck you, Reza. Fuck you and that short-hooded dick of yours! Here baby what else you need me to do." Moni replied.

"Grab a couple of them ties hanging up." Terrance forced Reza to sit on the bed. "Come on sugar daddy have a sit, we need to talk."

"How much money do you want? I have plenty of money." Reza pleaded.

Moni came back over by the bed. Reza screwed his face up at her. She avoided eye contact, wanting to cry. Although she couldn't, if she showed Terrance her true feelings for Reza, he was dead, yet Reza's words stung.

"Hurry up and tie him up tight." Terrance ordered.

Moni followed his instructions. Reza desperately wanted to spit at her. The force she used to tie him up assured him of his suspicions. He couldn't believe she was doing this to him.

"Alright now sit your greasy ass down next to him. You've crossed me for the last time." Terrance pushed Moni down and started tying her up.

"Babe, what are you doing? I was going to tell you about him. I was just waiting till the time was right."

Reza started laughing. "So, you didn't plan this with him? He's your man? Like sleep in the bed with you every night? Does he know you're a prostitute? He still decided to be with you?" Reza turned to Terrance looking at him in disgrace.

"Answer the man. Did we plan this?" Terrance stated, also wanting answers to Reza's questions.

Moni shook her head. "No," she whispered with tears in her eyes.

"Am I your man? Do we sleep in the same bed every night?"

"I'm sorry, babe, let me explain." She begged.

"No. Answer the questions." Terrance demanded.

"Yes...yes...you are my man. The man I love." Moni cried.

"Stop. Don't start the bullshit. Finish answering the questions. Matter fact I'll do it. Yes, we sleep in the same bed every night. Most nights it's me, her, our daughter Jem, and sometimes our son. You know, the family she leaves at home while she sales her body. No, I had no idea she was a prostitute." Terrance concluded.

"Babe, I'm sorry. You wasn't working, we was struggling. I came out here with you thinking it was gone be like old times. But, you changed."

"You would find a way to switch this around and put it on me. Hold up, I'll get back to you. So, Daddy War bucks, where the stash at? I know you have some random stash sitting around."

"I have two million downstairs inside the floor of the fire place inside the library. It's all yours just take your girlfriend and leave."

"Two million? You just have two million laying around? Hold up, don't either one of you move. Let me go see if you're telling the truth."

Terrance returned with a duffle bag filled with money and surveillance discs. He sat the bag down next to Reza.

"You're a man of your word. I'm not sure if it's two million, but I believe you."

"Like I said please take the girl, the money, and leave."

"Hold up, daddy War bucks. You think I can just walk out of here with two million, my piece of shit whore ass wife, and you're not going to call the cops on us. Maybe you'll kick out four million to have both us killed."

"Listen you fucking broke bastard. I will never think, speak, or dream about you, that two million, or your whore of a wife. Just take it all and leave. I have a wife, a beautiful Persian with whom I love dearly."

"See, where I'm from you don't take, from a man and leave him alive to come back." Terrance grabbed a pillow and placed it against Reza's head. He pulled the trigger on the baby cannon, knocking his brains over the pearl white Persian rug.

Moni let out a high pitch scream, she was so nervous she wet herself. Snot dripped from her nose to her lips. Terrance grabbed another pillow.

"Damn, babe I forgive you. You shitted on me. I took you back because I loved you. I killed Jem's father and brought you out here thinking we could start over."

"You…you what? You killed Raheem?" Moni began crying a river. Tears flooded down her face and she became hysterical.

"You crying over that dead nigga? After he shot Kareem, snitched on us, and sent me to prison. You crying over him?" Terrance shook his head; his heart was broken.

"I love him, I'll always love him." Moni stared at the pillow and back at Terrance, she knew what time it was.

"Well take yo hoe ass to hell with him."

BOOM!' Her head fell right on Reza's lap.

Terrance laughed at the scene, "Just like a true whore. Dying with her head in a man's lap." He grumbled.

*****

Back in Mexico…

Laylah sashayed topless as the warm sand decorated her beautiful feet. Tropical fruits dangled from the trees as the sun started to set. Kareem lounged inside a cabana, watching two couples compete in water volleyball, in the small pool. Laylah had to buy him a dick ring, to stop his huge hard dick from getting so much attention. Now his hard on faced the ground. Women still stared, but not as bad.

Laylah approached, purposely blocking his view. She removed her skimpy bathing suit bottom. Her body still amazed him. It was obvious she'd had a little work done. Maybe a snip here and a tuck there. It was evident, also that she spent long hours in the gym to keep it tight.

Laylah dipped her feet in the water one at a time, cleansing them from all the sand. She averted her attention back to Kareem. Small beads of sweat cascade down his eight pack. Her nipples harden as she admired his dick.

She dragged her fingernails down his solid chest and rock-hard abs. Sliding off the dick ring, she released his erection, so she could test out those skilled hips. Then she straddled him reverse cowgirl.

"Ah, ssss…owww." Laylah moaned, holding the base of his dick. She rotated her hips in small circles, trying not to take too much dick at one time. She eased down further after each circle.

The top of Kareem's dick was covered with Laylah's slippery box. He felt her tighten and loosen her Kegel muscles, as she hypnotized him with her moves. Half of the residents in the Jacuzzi turn their attention towards them. Kareem, could no longer take the pleasure she was applying to the head of his dick. He removed her hand, clutched her waist, and slowly guided her fully down on his dick.

"Ah…ah…ah…sssss!" Laylah moaned louder.

She placed her hand on his pelvis, arched her back, and bent her head back. Her long curly hair tickled his chest, as she looked in the sky, trying to catch her breath.

Kareem grinded inside her, making half circles, forcing her to remove her hands. She placed her hands on his thighs and matched his thrust with a similar technique.

"Ah…sss…ah…sss…owww, yes kireto mikham."

"You want me to give you this dick, huh? You know I act out when you talk dirty in your native tongue."

"It feels so good babe. Ah…it feels, sooo… good!" Laylah arched her back again.

Kareem tugged on her hair, as she cuffed both her breasts, rubbing her nipples in the same pace as she moved her hips. Her stomach rolled with each motion, causing the onlookers to stare in awe.

"You love this dick?" Kareem asked.

"Ah, yesss…you know I love this dick." Laylah responded.

"Show me how much you love this dick."

Laylah leaned forward and grabbed his calf, making him bend his legs a little. She continued popping her pussy up and down his long dick, while taking his big toe in her mouth.

"Oh, shit." Kareem was baffled by the words that slipped out of his mouth. Laylah continued to perform her tricks.

Her ass bounced up and down on the head of his dick, causing it to bend forward. The awkward feeling of his bent dick and the sight of her dripping pussy, caused a tingling feeling to shoot from his toes to his balls. She sucked his big toe again after licking each one. Her body trembled alerting him that she was having an orgasm.

As her pussy juices ran down his dick she continued sucking harder. The tingling feeling got warmer. His leg began to jump. He closed his eyes and squeezed his ass cheeks. The feeling could no longer be contained. Kareem busted the biggest, hardest nut ever. He found himself breathing hard. When he opened his eyes, standing over him was the pretty receptionist from yesterday.

"I see you two are enjoying yourselves. It looks like the crowd enjoyed the show." She said smiling.

Laylah sat up and continued grinding on Kareem's dick. She wanted him to release every drop inside her.

"How can we help you?" Laylah asked, winding her hips looking directly into the receptionist's eyes.

"Sorry to interrupt, but you have an emergency message from a Maria."

A confused expression covered Laylah's face. She wondered why the live-in maid from her vacation cabin would be calling her, and not her husband. She felt Kareem's dick getting soft. She lifted and grabbed a towel. Wrapping the towel around her, she bent over, and kissed Kareem.

"I'll be right back. I told you I love that dick." She whispered and walked off.

N. TROUBLE

Chapter Eight

Kareem's flight landed forty minutes ago. Laylah on the other hand was forced to board one of her private jets last night. He had no idea how much money, Laylah, was worth.

Apparently, her family was third generation Shah. Not only was she smart, she was also rich. Not rapper rich or ball playing rich, more like Royal family oil rich. Her one-hundred forty million net worth, from the stock market was chump change compared to her true value. Last night while packing and crying uncontrollably, she also explained that in her country she was a royal princess. Her husband was the son of the most feared man in Iran. Their marriage was arranged since she was ten-years-old.

Kareem stood outside the airport waiting for Maxine to pick him up. A ghost, white Wraith cruised around the runway.

Little kids pointed screaming, "That's my car!"

Pedestrians squinted their eyes attempting to see who was behind the wheel.

The foreign came to an abrupt stop in front of Kareem and Maxine's tiny head popped out. "Come on, Babe."

Kareem was clearly caught off guard. He grabbed his small bag and jumped inside what felt like a yacht on wheels. He couldn't help but marvel at the comfort of the interior.

"This a bad bitch right here. What you took the Ferrari back?"

"No, daddy this was a present to myself. Our movie release is in two weeks. Mr. Perry gave all his cast members heavy Christmas bonuses, because nobody was able to spend time with their families for the holidays."

"So, you telling me you bought this and the 'Rari in what, sixty days?" Kareem shook his head.

"What the fuck? I don't see you in ten days. You just pop up asking me to pick you up from the airport. After you been who knows where, with who knows who, and you drilling me about buying a car with *my* money?"

"Look, you right it's your money. I promise not to speak one word about what you do with your money again. Just don't say I never tried to teach you."

"Who are you fucking, Kareem?" Maxine questioned, getting back to the importance of the conversation.

"What?" Kareem, asked acting shocked.

"Who are you giving my dick, too? And don't lie." Maxine repeated her voice filled with attitude.

"Why you asking me that?" Kareem argued.

"Come on you know, I'm not one of those slow bitches. We have been totally honest with each other this long. Like I told you before. I know I'm not the only woman in your life, but I was cool with at least being number one. Not only are you giving my dick away. You broke the number one rule you had us both agree on. Nobody gets our heart but us. So, tell the truth. You didn't kiss me, tell me how sexy I looked, or even let me know that you missed me. You just got right in talking shit, so who is she?"

Kareem sat there feeling confused. He'd always made it his business, to compliment every woman he's ever been with since he was younger. It was the one thing his uncle taught him that stuck. He wondered, if what Maxine was saying was true. Did he allow Laylah to steal his heart?

"So now your shy? I'm a big girl now. You can tell me the truth. Who knows if she's pretty enough, you might can have us both, because I'll be damned if I'm letting you go." Moni stated.

"Yeah, I've been seeing somebody else weekly. She's married, well was married." Kareem admitted, shaking his head, thinking about Laylah.

He pulled out his phone to send her a text, asking if she was okay, letting her know he was back, and to call if she needed anything even to just talk.

"So, who is she? Where you meet her at? It's not that bitch, Tender, is it? Because I'll beat that bitch up, in front of her husband."

"Nah, my profes…oh shit. What the fuck? Yo, take me to Terrance's house."

"Why what's the matter. I still want some dick. You not about to play me like I'm just some Uber driver or…"

Kareem cut her off. "Yo, chill the fuck out. Terrance just text me saying Moni got killed. I gotta go holla at him."

"Moni? Why that name sound familiar?" Maxine asked.

"She the one that helped my ex-wife, steal all our money." Kareem told her. while giving her a knowing look.

"Nah, that's not it. I heard that name recently. I just can't pin point where. And Terrance brought that bitch out here after all that? Pardon the dead, but it sounds like maybe she got what she deserved."

Kareem just shook his head. Maxine said what he was already thinking.

****

Back at Terrance's Apartment...

Terrance consoled his son as tears poured down his young cheeks. He had been crying non-stop since discovering what happened to his mother, while watching the news.

Terrance was called down to identify the body. Unable to contact Kareem or Moni's friend, slash co-worker Shanae. He was forced to call Heather and Lisa, over to watch the kids while he went to the morgue. On his visit, he ran into the most beautiful exotic looking woman he'd ever seen. He heard the Detectives saying she was the wife of the male victim found with Moni.

Reexplaining to Lil' Terrance what happened, and why the news reporter had slandered Moni's name. By labeling her a prostitute, escort, or high-class hooker, was heartbreaking. Heather and Lisa cleaned up, while Shanae kept Jem busy. She had just arrived this morning after seeing the news also.

"So, Terrance are you going to have Moni's body shipped back to Jersey?" Shanae asked.

Lil' Terrance started bawling again, snot dripped from his nose, as he caught hiccups.

"Shanae, I don't think this is the appropriate time to talk about that. Don't you see he's taking this very hard?" Heather interrupted.

"Who are you, again? I don't even recall my friend, Moni ever mentioning either of you. So, please don't come in here telling me what to ask or say when it concerns my friend!" Shanae snapped.

"Just be mindful of the babies, that's all she's saying." Lisa added with just as much attitude, coming to her friend's defense.

"Ain't nobody ask you anyway…" Shanae rolled her eyes and pointed her attention back to Terrance. "Where's your buddy, Kareem? Isn't he Lil' Terrance's Godfather?"

Buzz! Buzz! Buzz!'

Heather went to answer the door. Terrance stared at, Shanae, making her back away. She detoured towards the bedroom, with Jem still glued to her hip. Heather opened the door.

"Oh, excuse me I must have the wrong apartment. I was looking for my brother, Terrance." Kareem replied.

Heather cracked a flirtatious grin. "You don't have the wrong apartment, Terrance lives here." She swung the door wide open.

Lil' Terrance heard Kareem's voice and took off running. He leaped into Kareem's arms, squeezing him really tight.

"What's up T-money Bags, I missed you." He rubbed his head, hugging him back, matching his young grip.

Terrance joined in for one big hug. He broke down for the first time. "She's gone bro…she's gone…" A few tears spilled from his eyes.

All the women in the house stared at the woman peeking from behind Kareem. Maxine's scowl caused Heather to look away. She could care less about who was mourning who, this bitch had just tried her by flirting with her man, in front of her face. Shanae, stepped around the men, feeling like Maxine's presence evened the battlefield, she invited her in.

"Hello, how are you doing? My name's Shanae, I'm a friend of Moni's."

"Maxine, I'm here supporting my *man*." She said putting emphasis on man.

Shanae tugged on her wrist pulling her into the apartment. Heather closed the door, rushing to stand back over by Lisa.

"What happened, Bruh?" Kareem asked.

Terrance just shook his head. Lil' Terrance finally released his grip at the sound of his mother's name.

He pointed to the television. "Look." He said, turning up the volume.

"This is channel 5 Eyewitness News, Reporting from Park City, Utah. Where residents of this upscale neighborhood, have been worried sick about the hideous crime that occurred last night. Two bodies were found in this multimillion dollar home you see behind me. One of the co-owners, Mr. Reza Al-Rekadi, son of the Prime Minister of Iran. Also, a real estate mogul and husband of Princess Laylah, who's a fifth generation Shah. That happens to spend her time on U.S. soil as a Professor at the University of Utah. While maintaining an impressive stock portfolio that has the big names on Wall Street knocking on her door.

The other victim was Moni Carter. Who authorities say worked for the Salt Lake City Post Office by day, and a high-class escort service by night. Still residents say they're ready to pack up and put their homes on the market. Park City was always known as an affluent neighborhood, where the wealthy came to vacation, and have fun. Now it's no longer the place to die for, no pun intended. This is, Jean Shanti Irving, signing off."

"I knew I'd heard that name before. They been playing this on all the news stations all day. They don't know who or why they got killed. Sounds like ole' buddy wife might of..."

"Maxine!" Kareem had to silence her.

Everybody including Lil' Terrance was staring at her like she was crazy.

"I'm just saying...you know what? I'll be in the car. I know when I'm not wanted. Sorry for your loss." Maxine motioned towards the door.

Kareem was stuck, Laylah's husband was messing around with Moni. Who happened to be an escort and they both ended up dead. He stared at Terrance, who had a nonchalant look on his face.

"Damn, did Terrance kill them? He is crazy as hell. I don't see Laylah having this done. She's too sweet. Maxine doesn't know what she's talking about." Kareem said to himself. His phone went off alerting him of Laylah's reply to his text. He quickly opened the message.

//: *Yes, I'm home. All of my family are flying in tonight. Thanks for all the support, but I cannot do this with you right now. Please do not call or text me for a while. I have to honor my husband's death and get our finances in order. If either one of our families find out about you and me. I would lose everything and be cast from everything I love. Please understand where I'm coming from, I'll contact you when I'm ready.*

Kareem read the message twice. He started to respond back asking for a better explanation, before realizing she'd given him all he needed to know. They come from different cultures and she had a lot to lose by messing around with him in the first place.

"Look bruh, I just got back. Let me go home take a shower, eat, rest, and I'll be back as soon as I get up." Kareem told Terrance.

"Can I come with you?" Lil' Terrance pleaded.

"Yeah take him with you. I'll finish helping the girls and start calling Moni's family. More than likely, they'll want her buried back in Jersey." Terrance said.

"A'ight, give me like two…three hours tops. Come on T-money Bags, get whatever you need." Kareem hugged Terrance one more time, then exited with Lil' Terrance on his heels.

Chapter Nine

Tables Turn

Lights flashed as dozens of camera phones and Paparazzi flicked pictures of their favorite actors and directors. Maxine stole the show in her see-through grey, ball gown draped in red rubies covering her private areas. On her arm stood the man of her dreams. Kareem, complimented her perfectly with his grey two-piece suit and red bow tie. He decided to come along to clear his head. He was stressed by everything going on with Terrance and Moni's death. Plus, he hadn't heard from Laylah in two whole weeks.

Laylah, being unavailable left a lot of extra time for Maxine. So, today he was there to support his woman. He'd finally agreed to make their relationship official.

Maxine waved to all the spectators and fans screaming her name. Her and Kareem, walked arm in arm down the red carpet. He peeked over and caught a glimpse of her in all her glory. He could tell she loved the attention. Her beautiful skin was radiant and her pearly white teeth, shined in the lights, as she gave the cameras her gorgeous smile. She carried on like a Grammy award winning actor and looked damn good doing it.

"You look gorgeous, my Love." Kareem complimented.

"Thank you." Maxine blushed.

Her cheeks turned plum, in a way only Kareem could commit. As they entered the studio, they found themselves in awe of the decor. Hanging from the ceiling were gorgeous chandeliers.

The tables were dressed in silk cloth, with exquisite multi-color flower arrangements occupying the center. The room's atmosphere highlighted fame and fortune. It was filled with numerous A-listers, Maxine felt like she'd really made it. She placed Kareem's arm around her waist, as they strolled over towards the crowd, containing a few of her cast members.

Kareem instantly locked eyes with Tender. At Maxine's request, they hadn't communicated since that night. Maxine made it clear to them, that there would be no sneaky shit going on behind her back.

"There go our bitch. You want some of that tonight?" Maxine asked.

"Nah, Babe she bad, but tonight is all you. I just can't wait to get you home and show you how proud I am of you." He passionately enjoyed her lips, becoming aroused by the peachy taste of her lip gloss.

"Umm, why do we have to wait until we get home. You know how I get down. We can find us a little spot to get it on. You know I don't have on any panties."

Kareem just shook his head, discreetly rubbing and gripping her soft ass.

Back at Terrance Apartment…

Lil' Terrance had been handling his mother's passing a lot better. His family from New Jersey had been calling him regularly. His aunt would be arriving any minute now. Shanae, had made herself a permanent fixture around their household. She went to her day job and spent her nights helping with Jem. Terrance, still had Lisa and Heather, coming through every other day showing morale support. The apartment was spotless with all the women coming in and out. Meals were cooked, clothes were washed, and Terrance and the kids were always taken care of.

BUZZZ…'

The sound of the doorbell caused Lil' Terrance to jump up. He raced to the door and swung it open.

"Aunt Mina!" He leaped into his Aunt's arms.

"Hey, Auntie's baby. I missed you soooo… much. Look at you, all big 'n stuff." Mina said.

"Who is dat, Auntie?" Lil' Terrance pointed at the woman standing behind his aunt.

"Stop pointing that's rude. You don't remember auntie's friend aunt Vivian?"

Lil' Terrance stared at the lady and nodded his head. Back in New Jersey, he did remember his mother spending time with Vivian. He twisted his young face realizing, Vivian looked like an older version of Kareem's friend Maxine.

"Come on in, I'm Shanae, Moni's friend we spoke on the phone." Shanae greeted.

"Hi, how are you doing? I really want to thank you, on behalf of me and my family. You have been a blessing to us all. Lil' Terrance adores you." Mina responded.

"No need I'm just doing what Moni would have done for me."

On the inside Shanae felt guilty for introducing Moni to the night life. Mina stepped forward and gave Shanae a big hug. Vivian scanned the inside of the apartment. It was nice, but clearly, they hadn't been living the lavish lifestyle they were all used to.

Terrance came walking out of the back room with Jem on his shoulders. He stopped in his tracks at the half-hearted smile of Mina.

"Hey, brother in-law. Is that my beautiful niece?"

He didn't respond. A few feet away stood the woman responsible for ruining their lives.

"Wait, what's she doing here?" Terrance scolded.

Shanae was no fool the tension in the air, along with the stares, toppled with the moment of dead silence, indicated there was some bad blood between, Terrance and Vivian.

"Mama." Jem startled the whole room as she reached her hands out at Mina.

"No baby, I'm not your momma, I'm auntie." Mina collected Jem from Terrance's shoulders.

Everybody in the room stood there with blank looks on their faces. Jem poked her tongue out at Mina in attempt to play the same game she played with her mother.

"She's so cute, look at those eyes." Vivian said, attempting to lighten the mood and change the subject, but to no avail.

Terrance was still pushing the issue. "Why are you here?"

"Terrance, please…I invited her here for support. We know what happened, but right now it's about Moni and the kids." Mina interjected.

"She's not wanted in my home. She gotta go." Terrance stood firm, motioning towards the door.

"Terrance, please, for me…for Moni. Just let it go." Mina begged.

"It's all right, Mina. This is his home, I'll leave. Terrance, I'm truly sorry for your loss. I had every intention of coming out here, to sit down with you and Kareem. After speaking with Kareem a few months ago. I realize how wrong I was and know what I have to do to make things right."

"Not in front of the kids, Terrance. I'm going to take my niece and nephew out for ice cream and whatever else they'd like to do. Shanae, your welcome to come along. We'll leave you alone to calm down. I know you're going through a lot right now. It sounds to me like Kareem needs to be involved in this situation as well." Mina stated.

"You're right, Mina, I have something important to do. I'll meet you back at the hotel later tonight." Vivian explained exiting the apartment.

****

Maxine's Condo….

Stark naked, blindfolded, with both her wrist bonded to the bed post, Maxine squirmed in anticipation. As Kareem, dripped warm honey on her lips down to her toes. The scent of vanilla scented candles and honey fill the air.

"Let me lick you up and down till you say stop…" Kareem sang along with Silk as their voices soothed the room. He licked the honey as it slid down the bottom of her foot.

"Stop, that tickles." Maxine giggled, trying to move her foot.

Kareem grabbed her ankle and proceeded to kiss, lick, and suck the honey from her foot. Intently watching her reaction. He noticed Maxine arched her back when he sucked on her big toe.

"Oh shit, Papi…th…that's enough." She purred.

Kareem removed his lips from her big toe. He continued devouring the honey, while sensually sucking on each toe till he reached her pinky toe.

Maxine breathed hard as her breasts heaved up and down. Kareem glided his tongue across her inner thigh. As his thick beard, trailed behind sending a warm ticklish feeling up to her pussy causing her to get wetter. Her beautiful treasure stared at him. He used the tips off his fingers and lightly caressed the crease of her juicy wet pussy lips, then spread her open, and licked the honey from her box.

"Ohh…y…yesss, Papi. Yesss…uummm!" Maxine moaned, pushing her pussy in his face, arching her back.

Kareem glanced up at her pretty face knowing his intentions. He chose to prolong the outcome by sucking on her inner thighs and bringing his tongue down to the crack of her ass.

"Stop teasing me, Papi, please."

Kareem backed up, placed his hand on her stomach, and forced her back down. She tried to wiggle out of the bondage.

"Calm down, I got you." He blowed inside her warm tunnel before sticking his tongue inside her causing her to moan. He began alternating his assault, by stabbing her with his slow stiff tongue, then rapidly darting in and out.

"Oohhh my, gawd!" Maxine cried, grinding her soaking wet kitty into his face, rubbing her clit against his beard.

Kareem licked his way up her pelvic area cleansing her butter pecan skin of honey. Then he playfully made his way back towards her box, kissed, blowed, sucked, and paused. He repeated the same moves a few times, driving her crazy.

The teasing of his tongue running concurrent with the friction from his thick beard. Along with the pleasure of his strong hands, tucked gently under her ass. All the attention he paid to each part of her body, made her feel desired.

The way he handled her with every calculated move, he anticipated her every reaction. His tongue snaked its way up her stomach, to her large breasts. Maxine felt his thick, long, hard dick brushing up against her leg. It felt as though his dick was touching her kneecap and pelvic bone. Just the feel of the love of her life connecting against her soft skin, made her want him inside her.

"Fuck me, come on Papi. Come get this pussy!"

"Shhh, tonight I call the shots. You want this dick huh? Too bad. I'm not ready to give it to you." He sucked on her nipples, then placed as much of her DD's in his mouth as possible.

Maxine took a deep breath then blew out warm air, as she came for the second time. "I'm...I'm...cummming, Papi. Oh...oh...shiiit, Papi!"

Kareem twirled his tongue around her nipples, knowing her right breast and left big toe caused her juices to overflow. He found his way to her lips. They kissed each other passionately, as Kareem stuck the head of his dick inside her, then quickly pulled it back out.

"Please...Papi...please give me my dick!" Maxine cried.

Kareem slid back inside her going deeper this time giving her three, long hard slow strokes, before pulling out again.

"Ah...come...on Pappi. PLEASE!" Maxine whined, in between catching her breath. Just when she thought her prayers were answered.

Kareem snatched that monstrous dick she loved so much right out again. He masterfully massaged her right breast, while guiding his dick into her dripping wet pussy as his mouth found her nipple. Maxine's head spun, as all ten and half inches filled her up, his tongue seemed to work magic on her *Mike-N-Ike* sized nipple.

Engulfed in the pleasure and pain of his lovemaking, she unconsciously submitted. Kareem continued to long stroke her cum filled walls. He danced inside her pussy, moving his hips to the sound of the music.

"Untie me Papi, please. I just need to hold you." Her leg started shaking. An eruption inside her body occurred as Kareem ignored her pleas. He kissed her lips, forcefully grinding into her with a power she couldn't seem to remember him ever displaying. Each stroke was passionate and smooth. It felt like he had touched every spot inside her walls causing her to climax.

"Yes…yes…Papiii! Ohh, my gawd." Unable to hold onto him Maxine, wrapped her legs around him like a vice grip.

He gave her two long strokes, followed by three deep circular grinds repeatedly. Tears formed in Maxine's eyes, as she felt the music he was creating in her soul. This was the first time they'd truly made love and it felt better than she could've ever imagined.

Kareem removed the blindfold and finally untied her hands, still pumping away into her skillfully. Seeing the tears, he kissed them gently away. She grabbed his face and pulled his lips to her, kissing him with everything she had, communicating how she felt for him.

"Yesss…Papi…oh my…yess. I…I…I'm 'bout to cuum. Cummm with me, pleaaseee…cum inside my pussyyy!" Maxine cried, matching his circular thrusts, tightening her pussy muscles on his love stick, as they came in unison.

"Aahhh shittt…Maxineee fuck." Kareem grunted, as his seed spilled into her hard and long.

"Yesss, Kareem, give it all to meee." She said, working her hips and vagina muscles helping to drain all of his cum into her.

"I love you, Kareem. You hear me? I fucking love you from my body, heart, and down to my soul. I'm yours, I swear I would never cross you. I..." Her words were cut off by the feel of his soft lips.

She kissed him passionately, squeezing him tight in her arms as tears pour down her face.

DING...DONG...DING...DONG...!

The sound of Maxine's doorbell caught them off guard.

"You expecting company?" Kareem asked.

"No." Maxine answered.

DING...DONG...BOOM...BOOM...

The doorbell rang again, followed by banging on the door.

"Hold up, you sure you not expecting anybody? They really banging on your door." Kareem persisted.

"I know they got me fucked up. Let me see who this is?" Maxine maneuvered from under him, grabbed her silk designer robe, and headed for the door

BOOM...BOOM...BOOM...

"Who the fuck banging on my door like they the fucking police?" Maxine shouted, before swinging the door open, and her bottom lip dropped.

"Hey baby, how you been…you miss me?" Vivian said, as she stepped into Maxine's apartment.

Maxine was frozen in shock as Vivian tried to hug her. It had been eight years since they'd seen each other.

"Who at the door, Babe?" Kareem asked entering the living room, wearing just his boxer briefs. At just the sight of Vivian, rage overflowed every part of Kareem's body.

The smile she'd greeted Maxine with disappeared. She looked at Kareem, back to Maxine, then back to Kareem again.

"Did you just call her, Babe?" The look of pain on Vivian's face and in her eyes, was almost equivalent to the large amount of money she'd stole and the many nights he'd spent heartbroken in prison.

"Yeah, oh, you didn't know? My old bitch broke down on me. So, I got my mind and money right, and upgraded to a new, young, loyal version." He placed his arm around Maxine's waist.

"You piece of shit, I knew y'all was out here together. But, never did I think y'all was *together*. Silly of me to think you two kept in contact because of me." Tears rolled down Vivian's face.

Kareem started laughing, "Don't nobody, care about your crocodile tears. Where's my money?"

Vivian reached inside her purse and pulled out a check. "And to think, I had all intended purposes to give you back every dime. Then get on my knees and beg for your forgiveness." She flashed him the check written out in his name for one-point eight million dollars. Kareem reached for the check, but Vivian snatched it back, ripped it up in pieces, then stormed out the door.

"Ma!" Maxine yelled, attempting to run behind her.

Kareem grabbed her arm. "You better not, you always said you wanted her to know. Now she knows. Fuck her and that money. Her selfish ass left me in jail. She left you, her own flesh and blood, out in this world to fend for yourself. I don't know about you, but I no longer feel bitter. I feel better."

ON THE NEXT EPISODE OF

LATE NIGHT LICK VOLUME 4_{PRESENTS} HIDDEN EXSTASY

CHAPTER ONE

Two Months Earlier…

Shonda pulled up in front of the dark brown log cabin. She turned down Kelly Rowland's Motivation. She deaded her engine and parked in the designated spot he'd reserved just for her.

Shonda took a minute to enjoy the view, the beautiful, sunsetting illuminated in the flowing water of the lake, directly across from the cabin. The sounds of, birds chirping and crickets stirring in the distance calmed her spirit.

Shonda reached over into the passenger seat and grabbed her purse. She freshened her lip gloss and scented her skin. Shonda took one last look in her rearview mirror and fingered through her hair before popping the locks. She got out of the car, opened the back door, and retrieved her duffle bag and briefcase. As she slowly walked up on the porch. A sudden sense of guilt rushed over her, as she loudly knocked and patiently waited.

"Well damn, aren't you sight for sore eyes." He remarked after opening the door, admiring how her dark blue leggings looked as though they were glued to her smooth, caramel skin, showing off her curves and thighs perfectly.

"I could say the same about you." Shonda replied entering the cabin, unable to take her eyes off him.

He stood there covered in a large red towel, with tiny drops of water running down his chiseled torso.

The guilt Shonda previously felt instantly disappeared. Her body tingled and her pussy throbbed, as her eyes fixated on his dark cocoa skin.

"I had to jump in the shower, thought I'd be dressed before you got here, my bad." He responded rubbing his hand over his goatee.

"That's fine, Larenzo." Shonda answered, not bothered at all.

"Ok, well guess I should invite you in huh?" Larenzo joked.

Shonda tilted her head, and a smirk curved her lips, "Yeah that would be nice."

"Let me get that for you." Larenzo reached down, taking her duffle bag out of her hand, then he noticed her briefcase in her other hand. "I don't know why you brought that, darling? Trust me you won't be needing it."

"Well if my excuse for being out of town was going to be work related, I had to bring my work with me, Larenzo duh." She commented smartly.

"Whatever get your ass in here." He sat her bag down by the door in the living room.

Shonda shut the door and locked it, then followed him into the living room.

"I am all yours this weekend, baby girl." Larenzo faced her and dropped his towel, releasing his already hard thickness.

Shonda gawked at his nakedness. Before she could speak, he closed the space between them, grabbed her face, briefly gazed into her dazzling hazel eyes and kissed her intensely. As their tongues wrestled from one mouth to the other, he rubbed his hands over her breasts, through her long-sleeved, black sheer crop top, then let them travel down, under her skirt.

"I see somebody been waiting for me." Larenzo teased slipping a finger inside her wetness.

"I guess you been waiting for me too?" Shonda replied grabbing his manhood and squeezing it until it throbbed in the palm of her hand.

"Take your clothes off and meet me in the bedroom." He whispered in her ear.

Larenzo let Shonda go and turned to exit the living room. Shonda kicked off her shoes and eased out of her leggings and top. She moved quickly in Larenzo's direction stepping out of her thong along the way.

Shonda blushed and giggled when she entered the bedroom and saw all that he had taken the time to do just for her. There were scented candles set strategically around the room with small flames dancing on top of each one.

"Wow," she covered her heart with one hand and her mouth with the other.

The black and red silk curtains covering the windows blew lightly next to the bed. Her feet sank into the matching plush red carpet with every step tickling her bare-feet and toes.

Her eyes grew wide when she saw Larenzo standing in the middle of the room dangling a pair of red cloth covered cuffs in one hand and a black blindfold in the other hand.

"Welcome to your weekend." She teased as she pulled at the cuffs from both sides.

Shonda's stomach trembled when she saw the black, Queen-sized, the black sheer curtains on the canopy top was joined together by four mahogany bed posts with gold balls at the tip. On top of the thick mattress lay a huge plush red comforter which made her want to wrap herself in it. Her heart melted as she heard J. Holiday's 'It's Yours' crooned throughout the room, setting the mood just right.

The flames crackled, inside the red brick fireplace as the night began to get just as heated.

"You remembered?" Shonda's face lit up, as she lightly nodded her head along with the music.

"Of course, I told you unlike that lame you got at home, I listen to my woman." He remarked boastfully.

Shonda took a deep breath, "Larenzo if this is going to work I'm going to need you to refrain from talking about Roman."

Larenzo raised his hands in surrender, he wasn't trying to ruin the moment, he'd spent weeks planning for. "Alright baby girl you got that." He assured.

"So now what?" Shonda asked getting back to the cuffs and blindfold.

"Whatever you want baby…whatever you want!" Larenzo said taking her hand, leading her over to the bed.

As they walked to the bed they enjoyed the light summer breeze from the slightly cracked double glass doors.

Shonda was clueless of what the night would bring, she had many desires that she longed to act out. However, had never been in a position to execute any of them until now.

Here she was with a man who was pleasurably different from any man she'd ever known, including the man she loved.

Shonda closed the space between them, threw her hands around his neck, and feverishly tongued him.

"Damn you so fuckin' thick." Larenzo said caressing her thighs as he eased his tongue over his lips.

Everything about her turned him on, she was the perfect level of thickness for his taste. He grabbed her apple shaped ass, pulling her close to him. He could feel the nipples getting rock hard as her plump 38C breasts pressed against him.

"Don't worry I'm gonna take care of you. Do you trust me?" Larenzo said.

Shonda nodded nervously.

"Good now turn around." He demanded.

Shonda did as he asked and turned her back to him. She could feel the warmth of his six-foot two frame towering over her, and his breath on the nape of her neck, as he carefully slid the blindfold over her eyes.

After making sure the blindfold was tight and secure, he guided her over to the bed, onto the soft, red, silk sheets. As Shonda laid down she couldn't see anything except darkness, but she could feel everything he was doing to her.

Shonda's body tensed up as she felt the furry steel tightening as he cuffed her wrists to the bed post, she felt her legs being spread open as his cold hands caressed her luscious thighs.

"Relax baby, I got you," he whispered.

Larenzo's hands, caressed up and down her skin, mesmerized by her curves. "Damn you thick as hell." He commented once again.

Shonda's breathing escalated, as she felt him ease up between her legs. Larenzo's hands roamed over her full breasts, sucking, squeezing. He teased her stiff nipples with the tip of his tongue then rolled them gently between his teeth.

Shonda's body shivered as his hands traveled along her body and to her sweet-spot. He slipped two fingers inside her wetness and tickled until her hips began to ride to his touch.

"Mmmh…" Shonda moaned as his fingers plunged harder and deeper, causing her to become wetter and hotter.

"You like that?" Larenzo asked.

Shonda nodded. "Unh-unh...I wanna hear you say it loud and clear." He demanded and started fingering her even faster.

Larenzo twirled his two fingers around in circles, while flicking his thumb over her pulsating clit.

"Yyyess...baby I...I...like it!" Shonda moaned louder.

Larenzo knew she was about to cum by the way her legs began to tremble, so he stopped, and yanked his fingers out.

"W...why'd you...sss...stop?" Shonda questioned.

"It's not time yet." Larenzo replied. "Don't worry sweetheart, you will not be disappointed once I'm finished.

Shonda didn't say another word, she just laid there agreeing to let Larenzo have his way with her. She'd asked for this moment, and he was ready to deliver, so all she could do was embrace it, with no regrets.

"You scared?" Larenzo asked sensing hesitation in her.

Shonda nervously laughed, "Never scared, just a little nervous."

"Don't be, I got you...now relax."

"Okay...okay do your thang." Shonda answered.

Larenzo reached over onto the night-stand where he had placed a bottle of honey and a silver ice bucket. He opened the bottle, held it up, and drizzled it over her breasts, stomach, then all over her neatly shaved box.

Shonda's body was filled with goosebumps as she felt the cool liquid poured over her throbbing clit.

Once the honey was saturated to his liking, Larenzo grabbed an ice cube out of the bucket. Shonda's skin was hot to the touch, Larenzo knew the ice would be a perfect addition to his foreplay.

Larenzo rolled the cube of ice back and forth over her nipples attending to one then the other. Shonda's body trembled, and her heart drummed against her chest with every chilling drip onto her hot skin.

"Aahhh…Laren…Larenzo, it's…it's cold." Shonda moaned barely able to speak. Her breathing increased, causing her stomach to heave up and down.

Larenzo didn't respond, his hands eased down, moving the ice from her breasts, down to her belly button, blending it with the sweet honey. He repeated the motion until he was back up to her breasts.

"Oohhh…G…God…" Shonda moaned louder, her entire body shook, chills shot up and down her spine, and heat surged through her, despite Larenzo's ice cold taunting.

Larenzo, put the ice in his mouth, then began making his way down to her sweet spot. He held the ice on his tongue as he covered her entire clit with his mouth and gently sucked.

Shonda raised up off the bed, then back down, realizing she was incapable of going anywhere.

"D...damn...baby..." She squealed.

Larenzo's taste buds awakened, as the ice, honey, and Shonda's juices meshed in his mouth. Once the ice had melted. He licked and kissed her body, from her belly button to her breasts, from her breasts back down to her stomach, careful not to leave any passion marks, knowing she had a man to go home to.

Once he'd devoured all the honey, he made his way back down, to finish what he'd started.

"Oooh...sss...shit..." Shonda moaned, swaying her hips to the motion of his tongue action and finger thrusting. "Eat that pussy..." she shrieked, wanting so badly to grab the back of his head, and hold him in place.

Larenzo nibbled on her clit harder, plunging his fingers deeper. As he went from nibbling to intense sucking, Shonda's body started to convulse, she closed her thighs around his neck. Larenzo used the strength of his other arm and pried her legs back open. As he felt her about to release, he stopped.

"Www...what you doing?" Shonda panted.

Larenzo didn't respond, in a swift motion he raised her legs up on his shoulders and entered her slippery wetness. He slow stroked her until his iron hard, curved, dick was half-way inside her. As her pussy stretched to accommodate his length, he started fucking her hard and fast, hitting her walls intensely.

"Aaah...Larenz...Larenzo, work that dick baby. Oooh...God...fuck me!" Shonda screamed, working her hips, causing him to speed his strokes.

"Hell, yeah give me that pussy...that dick feel good huh?" Larenzo moaned. Shonda nodded, as he felt an orgasm rising, he stopped, pulled his dick out, and got off the bed.

Just as Shonda was about to say something, he put his finger over her lips. "I got this." He said, moving to the top of the bed, uncuffing her wrists, then to the bottom uncuffing her ankles.

"Follow me." Larenzo told her.

"Follow you where?" Shonda asked, sitting all the way up, snatching off the blindfold.

Her eyes followed him, as he exited the double doors, walked over to the square Jacuzzi hot tub, and slowly sunk into the water.

"Come woman, it's nice out here!" Larenzo said louder, stretching his arms on the side of the hot tub.

Shonda wasn't sure if this was a good idea. The breeze had gotten cooler since she first arrived, and her legs still shook from the euphoria she'd just experienced.

"Well I did say I wanted to switch things up." She reminded herself. "Alright I'm coming." She called back.

As she stood up, slowly getting off the bed, making her way out onto the patio, her legs were weak with pleasure. Once she managed to get out on the patio, Larenzo, stood up, took her hand, and escorted inside the hot tub.

Larenzo, scooped her in his arms, sitting her on the edge of the tub. Shonda looked up into the sky, at the bright stars and shining moon, as he started sucking on her neck. As she suspected the temperature had dropped, the heat from the bubbling water, masked the cold wind.

"It's so...so nice out here." Shonda stuttered.

"Uh huh." Larenzo mumbled, now sucking her breasts, shoving three fingers inside her wetness.

"Aahhh…" Shonda screamed, her walls tensed up and tightened around his fingers.

"Relax." Larenzo instructed. He took his fingers out, replacing them with his dick. He teased her center, slipping his dick in, then back out, repeatedly.

"Shit…Larenzo, you keep this up…damn boy!" She moaned slightly lifting her waist, to meet his strokes.

"Aarghh…this pussy feels so good." Larenzo, groaned lifting her legs out of the water, onto his shoulders. As his strokes intensified, he gripped her shoulders, and gazed into her eyes.

"Spread that pussy for me?" He requested.

Shonda reached under her, spreading her ass cheeks as wide as she could. Larenzo, plunged fast and deep, attacking her walls with precision.

"Ooohh…sss…shit give it to me baby!" Shonda begged.

"You want it all, huh?" Larenzo asked.

"Yes daddy, I…I want…want it all." Shonda confirmed.

Larenzo, gazed deep into her eyes, pushing all his inches inside wetness per her request.

"Shit I'm cumming in this pus…" Before he could finish he exploded.

"Turn around." He instructed.

Shonda didn't say anything as she quickly complied, stepping down into the water, turning her back to him as she settled into his embrace.

"You trust me, right?" Larenzo asked again. Shonda nodded. "Good girl." He replied, kissing the small of her back.

He pushed her forward until her back was arched perfectly. Larenzo tightly gripped the back of her neck. "Open your legs wide." He instructed.

Shonda opened her legs wide as he entered her.

Larenzo slammed all his inches deep inside of her. He kept one leg firmly on the bottom of the hot tub and put one leg up on the side of the hot tub. As he went to work inside her pussy, he released his grip on her neck, and held her ass, spreading it open. He stuck two fingers in his mouth, then slipped them inside her asshole.

"Aaah...uuunnh..." Shonda squealed, trying to move.

With his free hand, Larenzo pulled her back into him, fucking her harder, while twirling his fingers faster inside her asshole.

"Where you going...huh?" He groaned. "Stop trying to run, take this shit...you wanted it right." Larenzo said refusing to let up.

Shonda's body and mind felt like it was spinning out of control, she'd never felt pleasure of this magnitude.

"Aahhh…shit…you…you driving me crazy." She cried, throwing her pussy back into him. "That feels so fucking good!" She screamed.

"Whose pussy is this?" Larenzo asked fucking her harder.

"Yours baby…oooh…baby it's yours." She squealed louder, as her body quivered.

Larenzo pulled his fingers out of her ass and clutched her shoulders tight with both hands, pushing so hard inside her, his nuts slammed into her ass. He held her tighter as his body began to shake along with hers and they exploded together.

Shonda collapsed on the side of the hot tub, struggling to catch her breath, Larenzo collapsed on her back, letting his dick fall out of her.

"Damn your pussy good! Um…um Roman don't know how lucky he is!" Larenzo commented.

"What I tell you about that shit?" Shonda panted, shooting her eyes back at him. "Don't ruin a good moment."

"You right…my bad." Larenzo agreed.

Larenzo released her shoulders and she tried to relax as she was still wrapped in the adrenaline rush from their powerful orgasms. As Larenzo stepped out of the hot tub, he took her hand, helped her out, then scooped her into his arms. He carried her back into the room, lying her down on the bed, so she could regroup while he went to take a shower.

"You're free to join me if you want!" Larenzo called from the bathroom.

"Be there in a minute." Shonda agreed, letting her mind replay the night.

She knew she was wrong and that everything she was doing could possibly blow up in her face. However, at the moment she was in no position to care or complain.

Larenzo's dick filled her insides just right with every stroke. The orgasms he gave her were the most intense she'd ever felt, and unlike other men, he listened to her body and executed all her desires, no matter how big or small, no questions asked.

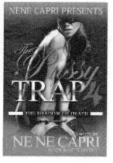

NENE CAPRI PRESENTS

1-CLICK

Google Play

Paper backs: Po Box 741581
Riverdale, GA 30274

C. ADAMS PRESENTS

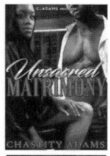

1-CLICK

amazon

NENE CAPRI PRESENTS

Available in Paperback..!!

The Pussy Trap series 1 -5
Trust No Bitch series 1-3
Tainted 1 & 2
Diamonds Pumps & Glocks
Late Night Lick Vol. 1, 5, 6, 8, 10, 11
By NeNe Capri

Chastity Adams Presents

Gangsta Lovin' 1 & 2
Love Sex & Mayhem 1 & 2
Treacherous Desire
Late Night Lick Vol. 2, 4, 7 & 9
Unsacred Matrimony
By Chastity Adams

We Ship to Prisons:
Po Box 741581
Riverdale, GA 30274